Grandmother's Fan

Sandy DuClos Eckart

SHELAH's BOOKS

ISBN 978-1-73-255720-8

This is a work of fiction.
The story and characters are fictitious
and are products of the author's imagination.

Grandmother's Fan

was designed by Daniel Franklin
and composed by Village Bookworks, Inc.
in Bembo, a typeface designed in 1496
by Francesco Griffo for the Venetian scholar
and printer Aldus Manutius.

This story is dedicated to all the quilters in my life, past and present ...

My grandmother Pearl, the quilter who inspired this story and who is reflected in Olinda; her mother, my great-grandmother Anna, maker of the original quilt the story is based on; my grandmother Nora, who made us many wonderful quilts throughout the years; my mother-in-law, Esther, who has graced our family's beds with the most beautiful quilts I have ever seen; and my mother, Alice, who has made lovely quilt tops and hand-tied quilts for her grandchildren and great-grandchildren to cherish.

Without their love of this craft, I would have never been inclined to write this book.

A Quilter's Prayer

A quilt is like love, made to last forever.
A bed without a quilt is like a sky without stars.
A quilt sewn together with utmost care,
Quilted with love is a treasure to share.
I count the stitches line by line,
And watch the thread record the time.
Love and memories we impart,
To quilt the fabric of the heart.
May the colors of your life be bright,
And the threads in your life very strong.
The best kind of sleep beneath heaven above,
Is under a quilt handmade with love.

Author unknown

PROLOGUE

My life started out in bits and pieces—literally. I first remember feeling "alive" after being stretched on a wooden frame one day. You see, I am a quilt. But not an ordinary bed quilt; I always knew I was special. I was loved and cherished for decades until I was put to rest, only to be reborn many years later. To fully appreciate my story, I invite you to take a journey with me, one that has ultimately left me content in ways I would never have thought possible.

PART ONE

I

My first memory was a dramatic one, from a time that was a notable moment in history. I remember loving hands passing over me and the feeling of something soft within. Sharp pricks, painful at first, eventually became a rhythm that I came to enjoy and realize as almost melodic. This rhythm sometimes accompanied music on the phonograph playing in the background, while those hands—those wonderful hands—poked the sharp needle through me and tugged ever so gently on the slender threads that would hold me together.

At the time, I felt almost peaceful as the work continued, eager for the final result, yet never quite realizing how beautiful I was to become at the hands of my maker. Nevertheless, I reveled in the moment as her swift fingers worked their magic. Most likely, part of the tuneful sound I experienced was from the slight singing of the needle and thread as it wove its way through me, up and down, several stitches at a time, steadily working its way across my form.

Suddenly, a soft thump was heard from somewhere nearby. I felt her hands push against me to steady herself as she got up from the chair she was sitting in. I could hear a door opening, then a crinkling, rustling sound. A few moments later, a gasp came from her lips. After a while, I heard the sound of her footsteps coming back into the room. She sat down once more, but instead of picking up the needle again, she rested her hands on me and seemed to gather them into each other. I knew not what she was doing, but I heard faint mumblings, the words of an ancient devotion coming from her mouth. How odd that I, such as I was, stretched on boards and consisting of only soft cotton and fabric, could hear and feel such things! I marveled at that for a moment, until her hands found the needle and thread and continued stitching the wondrous thing that was to become me.

A short time later, a loud knock at the door alerted the woman, and once again I felt her raise herself from her seat. I heard another voice, distant at first, but then I felt the woman's presence as she sat back in her chair. Her visitor had followed her into the room and was offered a chair nearby. The pair talked softly, almost reverently, about the story they had just read in the newspaper about a great ship, the *Titanic,* bound for New York from Southampton, England. It had sunk after hitting an iceberg near Newfoundland.

Anna, it seemed, was the name of my creator. She and the other woman, whom she called Mrs. Tarantina, talked about how sad it made them to hear this awful news. They went on to say that although they knew not a single passenger who was aboard this ship, they wondered about them ... and not only the passengers, but their families, and how wretched it would have been for the shipwrecked survivors to be stranded in the cold water. The article had said that while there were some who had lived and been rescued, stranded in lifeboats and pulled from the frigid sea, many others had perished. The two women wondered why more people weren't saved, and why, as the news story had stated, some of the boats were only half-filled.

Just as before, Anna's hands joined in prayer, as she murmured soft words of God and Peace and Lost Souls. The other woman, Mrs. Tarantina, joined Anna and after a time, she began to help Anna work her magic on me.

This newcomer and Anna seemed to know each other very well. They spoke in soft tones; Anna's voice was calm and soothing to me, yet her friend was often difficult to understand. She had a different manner of speaking than Anna did; her words often ran together, and her speech had a slightly foreign twang. I found it fascinating that I could understand what they were saying and wondered how this was even possible.

The conversation between the two soon turned more domestic. Anna explained to Mrs. Tarantina how long it had taken her to piece the top of this quilt she was working on. That is how I learned what I was called—a quilt. What a lovely name! She went on to say that she used scraps from her husband's old shirts, her daughter's now too-small dresses, and a tattered old jacket that had been worn by one of her sons. Why, there were even pieces of her abandoned aprons that could no longer be useful, feed sacks that had been emptied, and her children's christening gown. It had taken her most of the past year to stitch all the pieces together by hand, because she did not yet own a sewing machine. My, it made me proud to hear that some of all those things was included in me!

The pattern, she explained, was called "Grandmother's Fan." When Mrs. Tarantina asked Anna why she had chosen this particular pattern, Anna said that she just liked it. She continued, saying that she didn't remember her grandmother very well, because she had passed away when Anna was barely three years old. In a way, it was a sort of tribute to her.

Mrs. Tarantina replied that she had heard just yesterday that the price of cotton was going up again. She said Anna had better be glad she had bought hers for this quilt when she did. Anna just nodded in silence, realizing that she had not yet admitted to her husband, Edward, that she had spent some of her household money on the cotton. It was the only thing she had needed to purchase besides the thread, since all the other cloth was from scraps.

She said as much to the older woman, who replied that as frugal as Anna was elsewhere in her everyday expenses, she was certain that Edward would not make a fuss. After all, a quilt was a necessity that would keep them warm in the winter, not an extravagance.

As the morning went on, the two stitched on me as they talked about the town of Parrie in which they lived. They chattered about their church friends, neighbors, and mutual acquaintances—mostly general small talk. Eventually, Anna invited Mrs. Tarantina to join her for a bite to eat, asking if she wouldn't like a sandwich of fresh baked bread with summer sausage and a slice of peach pie. The peaches, Anna told her visitor, were the final jar from what she had canned last summer—grown on the trees in her own small fruit orchard.

After their meal, Anna asked Mrs. Tarantina if she would like to walk outside so they could stretch their legs and take in the early spring day. I heard them leave the front room, and a quiet settled over the house.

After their break outside, they had to roll me up somewhat on the quilt frame. I assumed this was so they could reach a new spot to stitch. Not long after that, Mrs. Tarantina announced that she'd better get home, as a friend was coming into town for a visit the next day and she wanted to set some dough to rise so she could bake rolls in the morning. She invited Anna to join them, but Anna was vague, saying that the next day was wash day again, and she had some baking to do herself.

Mrs. Tarantina left, with a reminder that if Anna changed her mind, she was more than welcome to drop by. She then made her way out the door and closed it with a click. Anna, deep in thought, realized that Mrs. Tarantina was quite a good friend, but one she really knew very little about, since she rarely spoke about her past. I came to realize that Anna and I had quite a connection, for she wasn't speaking these thoughts out loud. Why all these things were happening to me, I did not know, but I relished the idea that I was able to understand her thoughts.

Anna knew that Mrs. Tarantina was from the South, and when she had arrived in town with her husband, most locals had a hard time understanding her lilting Southern dialect. Anna, who was used to her peculiar speech by now, barely noticed anymore. When people referred to her, she was always called Mrs. Tarantina or simply "the Mrs."—the name her husband had used for her.

When Mrs. Tarantina and her husband had come to Parrie, she told everyone what her first name was, but no one could remember it or even begin to pronounce it. Most were too embarrassed to keep asking her to say it again. Her husband, God rest his soul, had gone by the name of Heiney, which Anna thought might be a nickname for Henry, but she wasn't sure. Anna just knew that the Mrs. was a good friend, often loaning her household items or offering to help with the children. The Tarantinas didn't have any children of their own.

Last year, Heiney died from pneumonia after falling into the river trying to retrieve his fishing nets one late winter day. The Mrs. had taken to coming over quite often after that. With him gone more than a year now, Anna realized that she was probably lonely for company. A short while after he had passed on, Anna had asked her if she would be moving back down South, but the Mrs. said she had no one to go back to, that her family members were all long dead, and Parrie had been her home now for a long time.

Another question Anna and most of the people in town had was about Mrs. Tarantina's age. The Mrs. had never offered this tidbit of information to her, and Anna thought it rude to ask. She speculated that the Mrs. was probably around her own mother's age, close to 70, but she was uncertain about that. Anna, 33 years old this year, often felt as if the Mrs. was more like a mother to her than a friend—occasionally giving advice, which Anna didn't always heed.

Anna's own mother, Mary, was busy with the family farm, having taken care of it for many years with the help of a local farmhand, along with Anna and her younger brothers, William and Daniel. Joseph, Anna's father, had passed away in '96, when Anna was 17 and the boys were just 10 and 7 years old. The family had worked hard ever since to keep the farm going. Now that the boys were older, the farmhand was no longer needed, but work at the farm left little opportunity for Mary to spend much free time with Anna.

Anna sewed a few more stitches on me, but soon I heard her sigh as she tidied up the various items lying on top of me: a spool of thread, a thimble, a pair of scissors, a soft ball of yarn, a piece of chalk that she sometimes marked on me with, and an old sock filled with fabric and tied closed for use as a makeshift pincushion. She went back into the next room where she and Mrs. Tarantina had eaten earlier and began other chores. I waited for her to come back, but since she did not, I assumed she must have forgotten about me.

It wasn't long before the door of the house flew open, and in came three more visitors. I learned from their shrieks that they were Anna's children, announcing that they were home from school and asking their mother what they could have to eat. Anna scolded them, telling them they knew it would be time for supper before long and they should go about the business of completing their homework.

Two of the children, both boys, said they didn't have any homework, because their teacher, Brother Francis, was not yet back from his retreat in St. Louis and Sister Cecilia Ann had to fill in for him. They went on to say that Sister was so old she sometimes forgot to give them overnight assignments. I wondered about that for a moment, but didn't have time to think long, because all of a sudden, I felt something strike me!

Anna cried out and told the boys to play with their ball outside and not to bother the quilt. I felt a warm sensation and I realized that she must have covered me with some sort of cloth—to protect me, I assumed.

I heard Anna talking to the other child, a girl whom she called Olinda. She told her to slice the potatoes thinner and to get a jar of tomatoes from the cellar. When her daughter clomped up the cellar steps and back into the room after retrieving them, she announced that it was the only jar left. Anna sighed, and mumbled that spring better hurry so they could plant the garden again, as they were running out of her home-canned goods. I heard sizzling and stirring and other sounds coming from the next room—the kitchen is what I had heard Anna call it.

The room I was in, the front room, as Anna had referred to it when Mrs. Tarantina was visiting earlier, was not a big room, but it was plenty large enough for the quilt frame. In this room, it did not interfere with the family's activities. The space was actually considered a porch with windows all across the enclosed sides. Since it was far from the heating stove, Anna used it only when the weather had warmed enough to spend a great deal of time in it.

The rowdy boys came back into the house, shoving each other and toppling over one of the kitchen chairs. Anna slapped one of them on the hands, and I heard him cry out. I was surprised that her loving hands would be used in this way, after they had so reverently prayed and quietly stitched earlier.

The boys, who I learned were named Wallace and Albert, shoved and hit one another and generally made a loud ruckus. Anna gently but firmly told them to go out to the chicken house and gather the eggs that they had not retrieved that morning, and to take the basket from the hook near the door on their way out. The boys returned outside, and Olinda continued helping in the kitchen, making clunking and tinkling sounds as she set plates and silverware on the table like her mother had instructed.

The kitchen came alive again when another visitor arrived. This one I came to know as Anna's husband, Edward. She offered him a cup of coffee fresh from the pot, and I heard her ask for the pail he used to carry his lunch in to work. They made conversation about the day's events, his work at the rock quarry, the sinking of the great ship, and the new chicks they were to receive later in the week.

Anna relayed her thoughts to him about needing to get the garden area ready as soon as the weather allowed, for there was need for more canned goods to line the shelves in the cellar. Edward said he would start readying the ground set aside for the garden and would go to Caldwell's Store on Saturday to get the seeds for it. Anna reminded him that she had some seedlings in small pots: tomatoes, beans, cucumbers, and squash, all growing on the window ledge in the front room. I realized then that I was sharing space with some pretty important inhabitants in this room. I hoped I would become as important as well.

My thoughts were jumbled as I tried to make sense of everything that was happening. It occurred to me that I, although just an observer, was witnessing life in this home as if I was truly a part of it. I marveled at all that had taken place in my short existence and was thankful for it, although the reason for it all was a mystery to me.

2

As the days went by, Anna established a routine when working on me, or so it seemed. She often would come into the front room and stitch a short while in the morning after Edward and the children had left for the day. Then, sighing with regret, she would leave to attend to her household duties. I could hear her scrubbing outside on a washboard, then wringing the water out of the clothes.

I couldn't imagine what she did next, because hearing and feeling were the only two senses I was able to experience. I could not taste, or see, or even smell my surroundings, and I doubted very much that I ever would. It was still a wonder to me that I was able to understand all that I could so far.

I assumed that Anna had to put the clothes somewhere for them to get dry enough to use again, but where I did not know. I could hear her sweeping the floors and washing the dirty dishes, cooking and baking, and I loved those sounds best. I could hear stirring and mixing, the opening of the oven door and the whoosh of warm air that would filter into the front room as she put in a loaf of bread or a pie she had prepared. All of these wonderful activities were not lost on me because, like I said, hearing and feeling were familiar to me.

When Anna completed her tasks, she would come back to me for a short while until the children came home from school. She would then gently cover me up, as she had that very first day, and sometimes she would not be back for a long time. I was lonely when she was not there, for she gave such special attention to me, but I understood that her family was most important to her.

Some days she was joined by Mrs. Tarantina, and on other days she worked alone, but very seldom were any of the children allowed in the room. One rainy day, Olinda came into the room with her mother. Anna told her that she wanted to teach her how to stitch on me. I was overjoyed! Of all the children in this house, Olinda was the one who most fascinated me. She was always helping her mother, doing things without being asked, and she was a genuinely pleasant child. Her brothers, on the other hand, seemed to know only the word "mischief," as I had heard Anna and Edward exclaim quite often.

So on this particular day, Olinda began to acquire the knowledge and skill needed to perform the craft of quiltmaking. I learned a few things about the family I had joined as the two worked together. Olinda was just eight years of age. She was quite young, her mother said, to learn how to quilt, but Anna felt it was important for Olinda to begin early. After all, Olinda was no stranger to stitching, having been threading needles and trying to sew clothes for her one and only doll for over a year now.

Anna was amazed by how quickly Olinda learned and how she was able to keep the stitches in a straight line. After just a short time, Anna proclaimed that Olinda was a natural and told her that anytime she wanted to, she could come into the room and stitch on me, provided her chores and studies were finished first. Olinda seemed overjoyed by that fact and clapped her hands together.

The two of them talked about school and Olinda's friend Minnie, who apparently lived just down the street. Minnie sometimes came home with Olinda after school or, during summertime days, went with her to the nearby creek to splash in the water. Sometimes, Olinda and Minnie went to play with their dolls at Minnie's house. The girls often tried to tag along after Olinda's older brothers, although it sounded like Anna discouraged that as much as possible. The boys (who I had heard Anna say were 10 and 12 years old) got into enough trouble on their own with their buddies, and she didn't want Olinda or Minnie to have any part in their mischief.

I learned that Minnie's only sibling was a much younger sister who was barely a year old, so Minnie didn't have any other regular playmates. Minnie's father, John, was the town banker. They lived in a large, beautiful home where Olinda loved to visit and explore the many rooms. Anna encouraged Olinda to kindle her friendship with Minnie, because Minnie was such a sweet child and because her mother had been very good to Anna and her family.

Minnie's mother, Adele, had hired Anna to sew dresses for herself and her two daughters. The payments Anna received for this had helped the family tremendously over the past year, especially when Edward was out of work when the quarry had temporarily shut down over the recent winter. For nearly two weeks, snow had been so deep that no one could even travel to work at the quarry, just a few miles outside of town. The money Anna had received for her sewing services had been their salvation, helping to put food on the table and coal in the stove. She would be ever grateful to Adele.

Anna told Olinda that of all the quilts she had put together, she thought this one was going to be the most special. When Olinda asked why, Anna said she hoped to save it for when Olinda got married. Olinda laughed, saying that she didn't think she was old enough to get married. Anna chuckled and agreed with her. She went on to explain that since she was using some of her best cloth scraps, it was going to be a beautiful quilt. She planned to only use it sparingly and to otherwise save it for Olinda's special day.

Anna said that she herself had received only a few quilting lessons from her own mother before her father died from a stroke at a young age. Anna's mother, Mary, had to work hard after his death to keep the family farm going. Anna and her brothers, William and Daniel, had helped too, until Anna left the farm when she married Edward. Now only William and Daniel helped Mary, since they were unmarried and lived on the farm with their mother. Work on the farm kept Mary so busy that it left little time for her to quilt. She was always tending to the animals and the crops in the field.

This was another reason why Anna had chosen Grandmother's Fan for the pattern, not only because it was a tribute to Anna's grandmother, but to her own mother, too, who looked forward to the day when she would have more time for the craft again. If taken care of, the quilt could be passed on to Olinda's own children, Anna's grandchildren. Olinda liked the idea, and she had just asked Anna what was to keep it from getting torn and tattered over the years if she used it too much, when someone came into the house through the back door.

Edward had arrived home from a visit to Caldwell's Store. He had purchased several items from the list Anna had given him, and she asked him to put them on the kitchen table. He told Anna that he had gotten the seeds they would need for their garden, but that they would have to wait a few more days for planting. Even though it had stopped raining now, it was much too wet to work the ground.

He told her that the new chicks were in a crate on the back of the truck, if she and Olinda would like to come see them. Out the door they went, leaving me to wonder what chicks were and if they would be bringing them into the house. I secretly hoped not, for if there were any more duties in this house for Anna to tend to, she would never see my completion.

When the family returned from outside, there was much conversation about the cute little chicks and how soon they would be big enough to lay more eggs than the old hens already in the chicken house. Edward said he hoped they would be ready in about six months, but maybe sooner. Wallace and Albert were designated as the caretakers of the chicks. Edward warned them that they had to be diligent, or the young birds would perish.

For once, the boys were docile and agreed to do their best. Maybe the added responsibility was just what was needed to settle them down, Edward told Anna, when the boys were out of earshot. The paper route the boys shared would not interfere, if they took turns and worked out a schedule between them, which Edward said he would oversee. Hopefully, the added responsibility would give them less opportunity to get into trouble with some of their unruly buddies.

Anna and Olinda did not return to the front room any more that day. I guessed the excitement of the baby chicks and having supplies to put away on their near-empty shelves kept them busy. Later that evening, it was oddly quiet in the house. Suddenly, I remembered hearing them talk about going to the family farm where Mary, William, and Daniel lived: Today was Edward's birthday, and it was time for a birthday celebration. I thought about that for a while, but since I had no explanation, I was unsure what all that meant.

3

The following day, Anna and Mrs. Tarantina came into the front room to work on me once again. Anna told the Mrs. about the previous evening and the birthday supper her mother had prepared for Edward. She said her mother was ever so grateful to Edward and the boys for helping at the farm when they were able. Mary had rheumatism, and she feared that in time she wouldn't be able to help William and Daniel as much as she needed to. Their farm was quite large, and it kept the two young men and their mother very busy.

If only her brothers would get married, Anna said to Mrs. Tarantina, maybe then they would have wives and children to help. Yet it seemed that was not to be. Neither of the boys spent much time away from the farm, so there was little opportunity for them to meet young women. Of the two brothers, William was the dreamer of the family; he longed to someday see more than just his corner of the world. Neither brother, however, ever discussed getting married.

The Mrs. asked Anna how old Edward was on his birthday, and Anna replied that he was 36. Mrs.

Tarantina said he was just a young pup, still not revealing her own age. Anna went on to say that her brothers had just finished planting the spring crops, so they had some time now to enjoy an evening with the family, and her mother had made a wonderful dinner. They had played cards—a few games of rummy and euchre—and feasted on a wonderful roasted chicken, vegetables, and fresh garden lettuce, followed by a delicious chocolate cake.

Mrs. Tarantina stayed only a short time that day, saying she had chores at home, but would be back sometime in the next week to help Anna again.

The next day was Sunday, and I heard Anna come in, clinking something in her hand and then laying it on top of me. Olinda was with her, and they talked about the morning mass they had just attended and how Father Duquette's sermon had been so inspiring. Anna was somewhat upset that they had gotten to mass a little later than usual, so she had not had time to complete her daily rosary before mass started. She told Olinda to go ahead and start stitching on me, but that she herself would finish praying the last decade of the rosary before beginning.

I felt a tickling feeling as the rosary beads crept across me, and I heard Anna's reverent whispering. When Anna had finished her prayers, she rose from her chair and told Olinda that she was going to check on the piece of beef she had roasting in the oven and that she wanted to add some turnips, carrots, and potatoes to the pot.

Olinda hummed softly as she worked. I enjoyed this immensely, having never heard anything like it. It was far different than the music heard on the phonograph Anna sometimes played during the day. Those tunes were mostly instruments. Sometimes there was singing, but never this throaty, reverberating sound coming from Olinda. Anna had never done this, and it made me happy to hear Olinda's soft humming. I felt so content!

With every stitch Olinda made, I felt that much closer to reaching my destiny—something to be admired and loved for years to come, as Anna had suggested. Olinda's stitches, though fine and straight, were not nearly as polished and exact as Anna's or the Mrs.' stitches, but she seemed to be doing a fine job, as her mother told her when she came back into the room. Anna inspected what Olinda had been doing while she was gone, and after having Olinda rework a few stitches in one area, she proclaimed that the rest of what she had done was wonderful for someone her age.

The days went by, and it felt like the room was taking on a warm glow. The plants that Anna had started on the window ledge must have left the room, for it somehow felt emptier, quieter. Anna seemed to work on me almost feverishly, as if pushed by some unknown force to see my completion. I had a feeling that as the days grew warmer, she wanted me out of the warm room so that she herself needn't be there either.

Finally, one day I had an odd sensation, as if I was much fluffier and fuller than ever before. It occurred to me that maybe I was nearing completion. It was quite warm in the front room, and some days Anna seemed to fan herself with something as she worked on me. I speculated that since they had rolled and turned me so much, and since she seemed to be working on only my outer edges, somehow her task was almost complete. Mrs. Tarantina came that day and helped Anna pull me out of the boards that held me, and they laid me across Anna and Edward's bed.

Anna told the Mrs. that she only needed to bind the edges of me, and she was so glad to be out of the hot front room with summer now fully upon them. The Mrs. helped Anna, so the job went much more quickly.

As they worked, the women talked about their flourishing gardens and all the vegetables that were beginning to occupy much of their time. Anna mentioned that she had already put away quite a few jars of pickles, beets, and green beans, and now the cabbages and tomatoes were coming in quickly. Later on she would be making chow-chow, a relish that her children and Edward loved, made from green tomatoes, peppers, onions, and spices.

Her peach trees were beginning to ripen, and preserving the fruit would be keeping her busy as well. The pumpkins they had planted a short time after sowing the rest of the garden were blooming, and some plants were even starting to form small pumpkins. Once they were harvested, Anna would cook them for pie baking.

She also liked to make another family favorite from the summer's end garden produce. Anna called it "Last of the Garden," another type of relish that included just about everything they grew all year. That, the pureed pumpkins, and preserving the apples from their trees were the final canning projects that Anna undertook each year. All in all, it sounded to me that Anna was going to be very busy soon and was probably relieved that I was one less thing she needed to tend to.

The pair stitched swiftly, and after a while, Anna proclaimed that they were finished. I cannot say I felt any different at that exact moment, but I did have a sense of something I had never felt before. Anna told the Mrs. that she had not noticed until today that Olinda must have pricked her finger as she stitched and that she had left a few spots of blood on me. She was rubbing something wet in the area, and then I felt them lift me and take me out of the house. Oh my! I had never expected this—to be out of the house!

They draped me over a line of some sort, and held me in place with wooden pegs—clothespins, Anna called them, as she asked Mrs. Tarantina to hand her a few from the bucket nearby. The two women went back inside, and I was left on the line so that I might dry. Now I knew what Anna had done with all the other clothes I had heard her scrubbing on the washboard; she brought them out here to dry and stretched them with the clothespins onto this very line.

A slight breeze stirred, and I felt myself lifting and dancing in the warm breeze. What a feeling that was, as if I was floating in the air! I could hear sounds nearby—buzzing and chirping and all the sounds of nature around me. Leaves on the trees rustled, and a dog barked in the distance. The train that ran alongside the town sounded its whistle as it passed by. It seemed much louder outside than when I had heard it from inside the house.

Soon I heard voices, Olinda and Minnie, who were playing on the back porch of the house. Olinda explained to Minnie that I was to be hers someday—not yet, but when she was older and went away to be married. Minnie announced that I was beautiful and wondered what was to become of me until then, for that would be a very long time. Olinda said that her mother had a rack where she hung most of her blankets and quilts; it was in the wide hallway in the house. Olinda assumed that her mother would put me there, and that I would be displayed on the rack and only used on her parents' bed for special days. She speculated that I might otherwise end up in a drawer or in the chifforobe to keep me clean till I was passed on to her.

I enjoyed hearing their voices as they played on the porch with their dolls, but soon they left to find some other pastime. Not long after that, I heard Minnie saying goodbye as she headed home, and Olinda went inside the house to help Anna.

A short time later, I heard the boys, Wallace and Albert, as they talked. Earlier that morning they had begun digging potatoes from the garden, then dumping them out and spreading them on the ground. As I swayed on the line, I heard Wallace directing Albert to get the sacks they needed to haul them down to the cellar so they could put them in the potato bin. All the while I felt myself floating, but soon I was still and the day grew warmer yet.

It must have been getting late, for I heard Edward speaking to the boys after returning from his workday. Soon he joined them, and they made quick work of loading up the potatoes to take down to the cellar. He urged them to hurry as it was going to rain soon, and he didn't want to have wet rotting potatoes.

A short time later, Anna came to fetch me. She folded me neatly and then placed me into a creaky basket and carried me into the house. It was much cooler inside. I realized she must have retrieved me just in time, for just as the family had finished eating supper, I heard the wind howling and thunder much louder than I had ever experienced before.

It was then that I felt myself being lifted and carried with a sense of urgency. I heard the children's nervous voices, Anna and Edward calming them as they went down into the cellar. Edward announced they would be safe down there—he had just seen the tail of the twister, and it was not that close, but they had to hurry. They had brought me down into the cellar with them!

Edward asked Anna why she had done so, when they had many belongings in the house more valuable than I, but Anna told him that since she had just completed me this very day, she was not about to lose me so soon. This made me feel so special!

The children huddled in a corner, and I heard Anna asking Edward to light the coal oil lamp on the post by the vegetable bins. The sound of the wind was growing louder, howling and whistling, and the door of the cellar was rattling, bouncing up and down so that Edward had to hold the latched handle tighter. Soon there was a pelting sound mixed in with the sound of the wind and the rain hitting the roof above—hail, Edward called it. It didn't last very long, but I realized how grateful I was that Anna had brought me inside the house. I had a feeling this hail would not have felt good on my soft form.

Gradually, the wind subsided, and the rain sounded slower and steadier. Soon they all made their way back up the cellar steps, and Anna carried me in the basket and set it down. She then joined the others who had gone to inspect for any damage from the storm. I heard Anna cry out that several of the peach and apple trees had broken limbs that would have to be propped up. Later, I heard hammering, as Edward and the boys replaced boards and shingles that had been torn off the house and roof. Then, farther away, I heard them hammering on some of the outbuildings.

Anna came back inside the house, and I heard her speaking to Mrs. Tarantina, who was with her. She told the Mrs. that Edward and the boys would soon be done, and that they would inspect her house for any damage, too. They both exclaimed that they were quite lucky that the destruction was minimal and that their homes were relatively intact—just a few roof shingles, boards, and broken tree limbs to deal with.

Olinda came back in just then and said she had finished piling all the limbs on the burn pit that she and Anna had been working on before the Mrs. came over. She brought in a few green peaches for Anna, telling her mother that she had only picked up the ones that weren't damaged or torn too badly when they were ripped from the tree. Anna said that she would let them ripen on their own, and that she was hoping the rest of the peaches on the trees would be salvageable. The Mrs. left when the boys and Edward announced that they were ready to make repairs at her home. Anna and Olinda then cleaned up the remains of their hurried supper.

Through all this, I sat waiting in the basket, content with the fact that I had been valued enough to be included in the trip to the cellar. I wondered what would have become of me if the storm had been much worse. My existence could have been very short! Little did I know that I was to have a very long history with this family.

4

· 1925 ·

For the next 13 years, I occupied several places in the home of Anna and Edward. Most of the time, I was kept on the quilt rack in the hallway near their bedroom. Once in a while, I was placed on the couple's bed, to be admired when friends or family came to visit, or as an extra coverlet on a harsh winter night. For the most part, however, I was left alone, to be saved for Olinda on the day of her wedding. All this time, I silently witnessed the everyday activity in the home.

Anna made many other quilts over the years. I heard her mention them, and she and the Mrs. went into the front room to work on them from time to time. Occasionally, Olinda would join in, but as the years passed and Olinda grew to have other interests, she joined them less often.

Names of the quilts they worked on—Log Cabin, Nine Patch, Dresden Plate, and others—would filter through the rooms to me as they worked. I never heard them say they made another one like me though. I felt that Grandmother's Fan must be something awfully special if I was the only one like that.

31

Some of these quilts, I heard her mention, she sold, and others were given to family members.

Through these years, the family weathered many hardships and shared many joys, and the children grew and grew. Wallace and Albert were lucky to have been young enough not to have been sent overseas to the Great War in Europe, but Anna's brother, William, had enlisted when he heard that strong young men were needed as servicemen. He told Mary that this might be his only chance to see the world.

She tried to talk him out of it, but he was determined to fight for his country, and he wanted to see other places beyond the farm. Unfortunately, there was nothing Mary could do, since he was a grown man now. She told him how much she would miss him and that he had better come back home safe. Sadly, William did not return. As a member of the American Expeditionary Forces, he was killed in France not long after joining up in 1917. It was several years before his body was found and returned to the States.

Shortly after the news of William's death, the family endured yet another tragedy. Daniel, who missed his brother tremendously, was driving the tractor one day on a hillside that had always been a nuisance to the farmers. He miscalculated his load, and the tractor pulling the wagon overturned, pinning him underneath. Mary found him later that day when he did not come in from the fields for supper.

Edward had stopped by the farm that evening to help Daniel move hay bales, so he was there when Mary came back to the house with the tragic news. Mary was beside herself over the loss of both her sons in such a short time. She was afraid that Daniel had been careless, for his heart had not been in his work since William's untimely death. The family, especially Mary, was grieving once more.

Anna and Edward, along with the boys, had been helping Mary maintain the farm after William left for the service, and they continued after his death. Now, with both boys gone, Mary had no choice but to hire farmhands to help her again. Anna and her mother prayed daily for the end of the war and were granted their wish in late 1918, when a peace treaty was signed and the troops were eventually sent home. This news helped somewhat with their grief over losing William. After his body was recovered almost five years later, having been identified by his dog tags, William was finally laid to rest in 1922 with a proper burial in the church cemetery, alongside his brother, Daniel.

Wallace, now 25, had married a lovely girl, Felicity, and they were expecting their first child. Wallace worked at the quarry with his father. At the time, the young couple was living in the house with Anna, Edward, and Olinda.

Albert, at the age of 23, was helping Mary at the farm the most, having moved in with her. He had offered to help his grandmother on a daily basis after William and Daniel had died, when he was still just a teenager. He often came home on the weekends to visit with the family and go out with his friends, but for the most part, he lived at the farm. He had courted a few girls, but was not yet married, as the farm left him little time for much else.

Olinda, who had just turned 21, was working at the new dress factory in town and had begun dating a young man named Lawrence.

After nearly eight years of trying to help Mary care for the farm while living in town, the family was finding things increasingly difficult. William and Daniel were both gone, and Lester, the farmhand who helped Mary and Albert, was getting too old for arduous farm work and was ready to retire. Although Albert had gone to live at the farm and help Mary, his true desire was to become a carpenter, and Anna and Edward felt that it was unfair to Albert not to let him follow his dreams.

Edward had grown up on a farm, too, and was no stranger to farming, so it was decided that the family would move to the farm to live with Mary. Her health had begun to decline and she was no longer able to take care of the day-to-day chores herself. Without Lester and Albert's help, she would need more assistance. The farmhouse itself was quite large, even larger than Anna and Edward's home. With the five big bedrooms, there would be more than enough room for the whole family.

Mary's hope was to someday pass the farm and all its land on to her only remaining child, Anna. With that in mind, it seemed the best option was for them to move there. Edward would give up his job at the quarry so that he could devote all his time to farming, and with the young men's help, they would continue the family tradition that had been passed down for so many years.

The family started packing up their belongings for the big move. Because Edward had loose ends to tie up at the quarry before he could pass his duties on to his successor, Wallace took some time off so he could help Albert with the harvest. Wallace and Felicity went ahead to the farm and took some smaller items out with them.

A few days before the rest of the family was to move, however, Mrs. Tarantina became ill. As I heard the story, it all started one day when the Mrs. was out in her yard picking up pecans. She stepped on a broken pecan shell that pierced the thin sole of her shoe, and the wound festered as she tried to care for it with her own remedies. Shortly after that, she started experiencing fever, headache, and vomiting. Anna, who was Mrs. Tarantina's nearest and dearest friend, brought her into their home and put her in Albert's old bedroom. She took to spending her nights and days caring for the Mrs.

During many fever-ravaged nights, the Mrs. alternated between lucid moments and speaking gibberish, while Anna bathed her with tepid water and witch hazel, one of her old remedies.

Old Doc Lemay had stopped by several times and said that she probably was suffering from tetanus, and that eventually she would have a locked jaw with body stiffness and convulsions. He had only seen this a few times before, he said, but that is what most likely would happen. He gave her what medicine he had available, but there was little else he could do for her. He said that he wished the Mrs. had called him sooner, when more could have been done for her. Now the infection had most likely spread to her bloodstream. He said the best they could do would be to try to keep her comfortable, because her illness was so advanced. I heard Anna's rosary beads clicking quite often during that time.

One night, as Anna tended to the Mrs., her friend spoke so clearly that Anna stopped bathing her to listen more closely to what she said. On this night, she made more sense than she had since the beginning of her ordeal. She told Anna stories that Anna had never heard before in all the years she had known the Mrs. She spoke about how she and Heiney had met in New Orleans in their early twenties, more than 60 years ago.

Heiney and his parents, Helga and Bernardo, had arrived on a ship from Italy when he was a small boy. His mother, a very unpleasant woman of Dutch heritage, and his father, a deeply spiritual Italian, were ill-suited to one another. Nevertheless, they had married, Heiney was born, and several years afterward they had come across the ocean to America, seeking their fortune. His father opened a small shop selling Italian leathers and dry goods, where Heiney helped him from the time he could barely see over the counter.

The Mrs.' own parents had died a short time before she and Heiney met. Her mother, Cecile, was an indentured servant as a young girl and had escaped from a harsh Georgia plantation owner. She had died after contracting cholera. Her father, Antoine, born in a backwoods Louisiana bayou, had been killed later that same year in a fire at the livery stable where he worked.

The Mrs. shared with Anna that she had had a wonderful childhood and that her only sibling, a sister, had died of consumption when she was quite small. Although her parents had been poor, she said they had never lacked for anything, material or otherwise. Love had been a constant in their home. She was so very lonely, having no one else in the world to spend time with after they were gone. Her work sewing hats at a shop on Canal Street was all that had kept her going. The Mrs. said she was still mourning the loss of both her parents and had begun spending a lot of time in prayer at church after their deaths.

One day at church, a handsome young man came in and knelt beside her. It was Heiney. After mass, they walked out together, and he struck up a conversation with her. The Mrs. told Anna that she was quite taken with this young foreigner, with his good looks and strange accent; he had the kindest eyes and the warmest smile. She explained that with her own dark skin, having been born a French Creole to her white father and black mother, she and Heiney had made a striking pair in the French Quarter. Heiney made her forget her sorrows, and he had her laughing at his jokes and stories.

The Mrs. said she had loved the man from the moment she laid eyes on him. The feeling was mutual, and they fell head over heels for one another. They spent time together quite often after that first day, and within just a few short months of courtship, he said to her, "Evangeline, will you marry me?"

Anna's ears perked up, for she realized that she had just heard the Mrs.' given name spoken, just as on that very first day she had met her. Only now it was as if she had heard it for the very first time, because the Mrs. was speaking in a slow and determined voice, and with such clarity. Evangeline was the elusive name no one in town could remember. She had pronounced it in such a deep Southern drawl that long ago day that it had been nearly impossible to understand: It had sounded like she was saying the word "eventually." Now it all made sense to Anna, and she almost laughed despite the grave situation at hand.

As her story unfolded, Evangeline revealed that she and Heiney were married at St. Louis Cathedral in New Orleans and had moved into a small house on Toulouse Street in the French Quarter. Those were the best years, she said. Heiney was working as a shopkeeper next door to their home in a small sundry goods store. She helped him keep the books and stocked shelves, while he waited on customers or took his buggy to the boat docks for more supplies. Evangeline said she could still see him, smiling as he greeted people that came into their shop, always so friendly to them. His hospitality spread by word of mouth, and people often came back just to buy from him.

Through it all, they had longed for a child, but it never happened for them. She said they figured that the Good Lord just didn't see fit to bless them with a child, but she never understood why, because they had prayed daily for such a blessing.

Several years later, Bernardo suffered a stroke and died. Helga, now widowed, moved in with the young couple, since Heiney was her only son. She then insisted that they leave New Orleans to go to a less humid climate, as the Gulf air was hard on her lungs. She had never wanted to come to America in the first place, but had done so at the urging of her husband. He had assured her that she would learn to love the new land, but apparently that had never happened, and she grew even more resentful after her husband's death.

They tried to dissuade her, because she was suffering from an unknown illness. They feared the trip would be very hard on her health. But Helga had her mind made up, and she said she wanted to leave as soon as possible, so they felt they had no choice but to follow her wishes. She had grown more bitter and more feeble as time went on, and they tried hard to please her. Evangeline said she had never met a more obstinate woman, had never seen another person as stubborn as Helga was. Heiney finally sold his business and much of their furniture, and he booked passage for them on a riverboat heading north.

On their way up the river to St. Louis, their planned destination, Heiney's mother's health deteriorated rapidly, and within a few days she succumbed to her illness. The ship's captain, who was superstitious about having a dead body on board, wanted to dump her remains in the river. He was afraid that she had had a contagious disease that could spread to everyone on board. He was not happy that she had been allowed passage while in ill health, and he blamed Heiney for the misfortune.

The young couple objected, pleading with the captain, who reluctantly agreed to hold off until their next port stop, after isolating Helga's body in the cargo hold. He said they had to be quick, because he did not want to delay the trip any longer for fear of an upcoming winter storm that lay ahead. He refused to transport her dead body the rest of the way upriver, and the couple had no choice but to follow his orders. Heiney hastily found a priest at the next port stop who agreed to say a few words. In a matter of hours, her burial took place in the closest cemetery Heiney could find—in Memphis, Tennessee.

Since he and Evangeline had nowhere else to go, they decided to continue the trip rather than go back and start over in New Orleans. During an unplanned stop due to problems with the boat's engine near Ste. Françoise, Missouri, they decided to get off the paddle wheeler to explore the area. Some of the passengers, including Heiney and Evangeline, journeyed across the river on the ferry to visit nearby Parrie, because a fellow passenger had told them it was a lovely area near the river bluffs.

The day trip, planned only to pass the time while the boat underwent repairs, turned into a life-changing experience when Heiney and Evangeline decided to make the small town their future home. There was a small store with a Help Wanted notice in the window, and Heiney convinced Evangeline that they should stay. He said this town just felt right to him. Evangeline shared with Anna that she told him she didn't care where they went, as long as they were together. They returned to the boat only to retrieve their belongings, and they never looked back.

Here in Parrie is where Heiney once again found work as a shop clerk, with Evangeline helping him as before, and here they established their home. They both came to love the town and never considered leaving. With the money Heiney had inherited from his father, he later purchased the store and its contents from the aging owner. They spent the better part of their married years together in this small town that they had come to call home. Evangeline said that ever since Heiney had died, she felt a part of her had gone with him, and she longed to be with him once again.

Evangeline went on to say that Anna had been the closest thing to a daughter in her life and that she loved her very much. She knew she was near death, and she said that when she passed on, she wanted Anna to have all her belongings. She even made Anna promise to bring Mr. LaFourche, the town solicitor, to her home so she could advise him of her wishes. She wanted to be sure that there would be no question about who should receive what she and Heiney had worked so hard for over the years.

The next day, Anna did as she was asked. Mr. LaFourche drew up documents so that Anna and her family would legally inherit Evangeline's house and its contents. Then he brought them to Anna and Edward's house and witnessed Evangeline's signature on them. Evangeline herself told Anna where she kept the keys to her home, and she wouldn't rest until Anna had retrieved them for safekeeping.

Anna thought that the Mrs.' first name, Evangeline, was the most beautiful name she had ever heard, and she wished she had known it earlier. She told Edward that she felt so sad that the woman she had called her best friend had lived most of her life only being referred to as an extension of her husband, not by her own given name. Anna took to calling Evangeline by her first name often as she nursed her friend in the final days of her illness.

A few days later, Evangeline passed away quietly in her sleep. Apparently, she did not have the convulsions or stiffness that Doc Lemay had warned of. I heard Anna cry out, and she roused Edward from his sleep to tell him what had happened. Anna told him that while Evangeline was holding her hand, she had looked at Anna lovingly, smiled, and closed her eyes for the last time. I heard Edward offer to go get the doctor to come and tend to Evangeline's body. They laid her out in the front room, where years ago the two friends had lovingly stitched me into existence.

When all was taken care of, Anna finally lay in her own bed. This was something she had not been able to do for almost a week, because she had set up a cot for herself so she could sleep at Evangeline's side. Anna stayed awake for what little was left of that night, crying softly, praying her rosary, and remembering her dear friend. I so wanted to comfort Anna, but such that I was, I could do nothing for her. I could only witness these events from the quilt rack in the hallway.

The final move to the farm was postponed several more days while the family prepared for Evangeline's funeral. Anna and Edward visited the solicitor, who gave them the deed to Evangeline's house and the necessary forms to be used at the bank. They were surprised to learn just how much money Evangeline and Heiney had saved over the years. Never in their wildest dreams could they have imagined that the outwardly frugal couple had saved so much money in their lifetimes. Anna and Edward were dumbfounded. It was quite a sum!

This money would be a blessing to the family now that Edward would be relying only on the farm for income and not working at his regular job at the quarry. Anna knew that although in some years the farm had yielded a surplus, in others it had not provided a very steady income to her mother and brothers. The weather and other factors all had a hand in successful farming, and many considered it a gamble. Edward and Anna realized just how lucky they were that over the years, Evangeline had become their friend, and now their benefactor. They vowed then and there that they would put this windfall to good use, helping their children as much as they could in years to come.

After the viewing by fellow churchgoers, neighbors, and Evangeline's few friends, a funeral mass followed at St. Joseph's, with the burial in the church cemetery. After those gathered had paid their final respects, the ritual concluded with a small meal at Anna and Edward's home. Father Duquette and a few other acquaintances attended. They all reminisced about what a wonderful person Evangeline had been. Several of the men recalled Heiney, too, and they had funny stories to tell, because he had always been a jovial man.

At the day's end, when everyone had left, Edward told Anna that he thought Evangeline was smiling down on them from above. I heard Anna crying softly, and saying how much she would miss her. Edward replied that it was probably best that they were moving to the farm. There Anna would have fewer reminders of Evangeline, because she wouldn't be seeing her empty house next door day in and day out. They made plans to go over to Evangeline's house and pack up her belongings the next day.

Since Wallace and Felicity planned to come back to live in Anna and Edward's house after the baby was born, a few pieces of Evangeline's furniture were carried over for them to use. Most of Evangeline's clothes could probably be used by Olinda or Anna herself, since they were about the same size. Dishes and household items were put into boxes so that Felicity could decide later what she wanted to use.

Since the family was not in need of Evangeline's house at this time, they intended to rent it out. Anna hoped that someday, when Albert or Olinda had settled down, one of them might choose to raise a family in Evangeline's home. For now, the rest of the furniture and various household items would be put into storage in one of the barns at Mary's farm.

There was one item in particular, a lovely trunk. Evangeline had apparently used it in her passage up the river from New Orleans, when she and Heiney had arrived in Parrie. On one side of the trunk was written her name, along with "St. Louis, Missouri," their original destination. Next to this was another notice with the disembarking stamp of Ste. Françoise, Missouri, once their travel plans had changed. The trunk had accompanied them on the ferry ride over the river to Illinois.

Edward carried the trunk across the yard to their house so that Anna could add a few items of her own for the drive to the farm. Anna realized that she had yet to pack me and a very old, tattered quilt, so she opened the trunk, checked to see if there was room, and carefully laid us on top of the contents. The other quilt lay beneath me as the lid of the trunk closed tightly. That night, Edward, Anna, and Olinda spent one last night in the place they had called home for so long.

In the morning, Wallace and Albert arrived to help load the wagons. The trunk was one of the last items loaded. Before heading to their new home in the country, Anna announced that she wished to go to the cemetery to say one more goodbye to Evangeline. She said she wanted to put a bouquet of mums from Evangeline's own flower garden on her grave. I felt the movement and jostling as the vehicle began its journey. It didn't take long for Anna to complete her mission at the cemetery, and soon we were on our way again.

After moving through the town and then up the steep grade of the bluff to the farm, I felt the vehicle leveling off and dipping down again as we crossed over the hills and hollows outside of Parrie. Then we must have arrived, for I felt the truck that was pulling the wagon come to a stop, and several doors slammed. The men lifted containers and furniture off all the wagons, the trunk with me in it being one of the first, as it had been among the last items to be loaded.

It was a warm, early autumn day—even warmer, as would be expected, inside the old trunk. It was quite stifling, in fact, and I waited patiently for Anna to remove me from the confines of the trunk. That was not to be though, because she must have had a lot of settling in to do. I felt the trunk being lifted and set down, but still outside, because I heard noises in the distance. These were strange sounds that I had only heard them talk about: cows mooing, horses whinnying, chickens clucking—all much closer than when I had heard them from the house in town. But there was also the calm quietness of the country.

The trunk must have been on a porch near the door, because I heard heavy footsteps nearby, tromping up the steps and through the door of the house whenever Edward and the boys passed by carrying furniture and cartons. I heard Anna and Mary directing them to the rooms or barn or shed where the items should be placed.

After a while, they must have finished unloading, because there were no more footsteps walking past me, and I heard Mary announce that it was time to eat. All was quiet for a bit, so I must have been too far away from the dining room to hear their mealtime conversation. Later, I could hear them all talking and moving around as they began to establish roots in this new place that they would all now call home.

No one came to move the trunk that day, and I was beginning to think we had been forgotten, this trunk and I, along with the rest of Evangeline's precious treasures stored inside.

A few days later, Anna and Mary came out to the porch, and Mary invited Anna to sit with her in a pair of rocking chairs there. I heard them talking about the past few days' events, and how everything would work out fine as soon as they were all settled in.

Mary told Anna she would be forever grateful to them for moving to the farm to help her. Anna said she wouldn't have it any other way, and that she, Edward, and the boys would do everything they could to keep the farm viable and to ease the burden of all the chores. She and Olinda would take over the household duties as well, and Mary could finally get some much needed rest. After all, Anna said, this was to be their new home now, and they were all looking forward to the change.

All of a sudden, Anna exclaimed that she hadn't realized that the trunk was still on the porch! She hurried over and opened it, letting fresh air flow over me. Oh, what a relief that was! Mary helped her take me and the old, tattered quilt out, and then they set both of us on one of the rockers for the time being.

Then Anna and Mary began to look through the contents of the trunk, commenting as they inspected what was inside. Anna found several useful items to add to the household—a handful of doilies that Evangeline herself probably had made; a pair of intricately carved wooden candlesticks that most likely Heiney had crafted, since he had often been seen whittling on the porch of the old house in town; and a beautiful porcelain platter, exquisitely detailed with small flowers and trimmed with gold around its edge. Mary told Anna it would be lovely to use for special occasions. Anna thought that was a wonderful idea, and she said she would put it in the china cabinet with the rest of the family's heirlooms. Anna carried these items inside.

The rest of the contents, including various articles of old clothing, purses, aprons, and outdated hats, were left in the trunk to be looked through another time. Anna was much too tired to go through it all now, and doing so was only a reminder that Evangeline was gone and that she missed her good friend dearly. Edward, she said, could haul the trunk inside and place it near the fireplace in the parlor, for it was sturdy enough to be used as an extra seat when needed.

When she came back outside, Anna gathered the old quilt and gave it to Mary, saying she could use it as an extra cover on her bed. As for me, Anna gently placed me back on my place of honor, the quilt rack, now located in a corner of the parlor. I was overjoyed to be back where I belonged! At this point, I wished so much to not only hear and feel, but also to see my new surroundings. To me, this seemed very elusive, and I wondered if it would ever happen.

Long ago, shortly after my birth, I had heard Anna helping a young Olinda with her studies, and they were talking about the five senses. I had listened at that time, and apparently these consisted of hearing, touching, tasting, smelling, and seeing. Over the years, I came to realize that I could hear and that I had the feeling sense of touch. Although I myself could not touch, I could feel others touch me, and I had the feeling of new surroundings when my form was moved or rearranged. For a long time that was enough for me, but now I longed for more.

As for tasting, I realized that this was something I would probably never experience, for I was rarely around the food that others seemed to need for nourishment. I didn't care about this because I felt so stuffed full already.

The sense of smell was not as important to me either. I had learned that not everyone had the same sense of smell. For example, Anna often exclaimed that she didn't care for the scent of Edward's pipe when he smoked it, but he said that the smell didn't bother him at all. I assumed this meant that he couldn't smell it. Although it would be wonderful to enjoy the aromas of Anna's fresh baked goods or the flowers she said she brought in from the garden, it didn't matter to me very much that I couldn't.

What did matter to me was that everyone I had come in contact with so far had been able to see, and I always wanted to be able to see, too. I heard them describe the lovely landscape around them, the turning of the trees to wondrous colors in autumn, the winter's first snow, the brilliance of blooming flowers in the spring, and the crops as they pushed through the gardens and fields in the spring and summer. I had heard descriptions of all of these things from the family, and I longed to experience them myself.

Most of all, I hoped that someday I would be able to look into the faces of Anna and her family, view the rooms that I occupied, and—no matter where I was—see all that surrounded me. Until that day came, if it ever did, I found myself yearning for it to happen.

The autumn days were growing shorter. I could feel the breezes coming in through the windows and doorways when they were open, and there was a sharper bite to them, as if winter was just around the corner. Edward and the boys were busy in the fields harvesting crops, and Felicity was patiently awaiting the baby's arrival. Doc Lemay had said that it would be any day now.

One unseasonably warm day after Sunday mass, Olinda announced that Lawrence was coming for a visit; he would be taking her on a picnic near his family's home by the river, and she asked Anna if she could pack some food to take along. Anna helped her make sandwiches from the ham she and Mary had baked the day before, and they placed them in a basket, along with a few apples picked from the trees in the yard. Olinda added a jar of tea they had brewed outside in the sun.

After Lawrence arrived and they were preparing to drive off, Olinda rushed back into the house to ask Anna if they could take a blanket along so they would have something to sit on for their picnic. Anna told her it was time to try out the new quilt, as long as she promised to set it in the high grass—not too near the river bank, where it would get soiled. Olinda promised she would take good care of me.

I felt Olinda lift me off the quilt rack and carry me out to Lawrence's car. I could not believe I was heading out for an adventure away from the farm! Now would be the perfect time to see my surroundings, but I seriously doubted that this would happen.

On the way, Lawrence explained that the best way to get to his family's home near the river, a few miles outside of town, was to travel on the hard road for a while, then head across to the dirt track that led to the river. As they drove along, Olinda asked Lawrence questions about the homes on stilts she saw as they approached the river. He told her they were built this way so that when the banks swelled from heavy rains, the homes wouldn't flood.

Olinda told Lawrence that she had only ventured out this way once. It was when she was a child, and she had gone with her father to purchase firewood at one of the houses they passed earlier. She asked Lawrence how much farther they were going, and he told her that they would actually be going just a little past his house. It was the last house up ahead, just before a small bend in the river where his father's makeshift lighthouse was located.

Lawrence explained that his father was an official lamplighter for the Corps of Engineers, and it was his responsibility to light fires for the large boats and barges along the river to make sure they could see the sharp bend and not run aground. He performed these duties part-time, as needed. That, along with farming, was his father's livelihood.

Lawrence had established himself first as a deckhand, and more recently as a riverboat pilot. He was pleased to tell Olinda all about his adventures as he drove the car alongside the river. He had spent many days and nights on the waterway, and he enjoyed it immensely. Lawrence said that a few of his older brothers were already working as boat pilots, and one of his younger brothers hoped to become one as well.

Listening to the young couple talk, I could tell they were very much in love. Although Olinda had not brought Lawrence home more than a handful of times, I suspected from their conversation that they had met quite often in town. This was her first visit, however, to Lawrence's home.

Lawrence told Olinda that he had quite a few brothers and sisters—eight, in fact—and that their home was nothing like Olinda's. He said the boys all shared one room and the girls another. His parents' room was downstairs, close to the living and kitchen area. Only two of his siblings were married, so the quarters were still fairly cramped. Lawrence said that as soon as he could save enough money, he wanted to move into a place of his own near the ferry landing and docking station, so that the commute to his boat would be even shorter.

Finally, Lawrence pointed out his family's home. He said they would stop in for a short visit on their way back, before he took Olinda back to the farm. Lawrence said the family was probably just sitting down to their own noon meal, and there was so much chaos in the house during mealtime that he didn't want to scare Olinda off. She retorted that she was sure that couldn't happen, but he kept on driving all the same.

Just past his home, Lawrence remarked that down below the high riverbank, where the land jutted out, was the point where his father's fires burned on foggy nights. Olinda said she could see the fire pits and the wood pile nearby. She had a good view, she said, because the road was much higher than the river; it had been such a dry summer that the river was fairly low.

Olinda and Lawrence talked for a bit about the flood a few years ago, and he mentioned that they had to use boats to get out of the stilt houses that year. He also explained that his father didn't need to light fires during times of high water, like he did when the river was low.

Just after the bend in the river, Lawrence said he would pull the car off near a small group of trees, because he thought that would be a good spot for a picnic lunch. They both got out, and I felt strong arms lift me and the picnic basket up in one swift motion. It wasn't a long walk, apparently, for I was soon resting on a new surface, one that I had never experienced before.

Olinda mentioned how thick and high the grass was, so I realized I was lying on grass. It felt soft and prickly at the same time. The grass was dry, and the sun coming through the trees was warm, even for this time of year. Lawrence mentioned that we must be experiencing Indian summer, because the day was really getting warm. He suggested that maybe he and Olinda could walk down to the riverbank later and stick their toes in the water for a while. Olinda said that sounded like a nice idea, as long as the water wasn't too cold.

Olinda and Lawrence made themselves comfortable on me. They enjoyed their picnic lunch and shared the jar of tea. I felt at the time that if I was meant to experience the sense of tasting, it would have happened that afternoon, because they were consuming food right on top of me. This was not on my wish list though, because I was still so full of the soft cotton inside me that I never experienced hunger of that nature. In any case, I did not acquire the sense of taste that day.

While they ate, they shared casual conversation about mutual friends, their families, and their jobs.

Once they were finished, they packed up the basket and set it aside. Then they both stretched out to relax. I could feel the sun's warmth, and it was getting warmer with each passing moment. As the pair rested on top of me, I could barely make out their quiet voices. There were new sounds all around me: I could hear the sound of the river lapping lazily at the bank, a few birds chirping, and a bee buzzing nearby. Lawrence tried to swat it—apparently it had nearly gotten caught in Olinda's hair.

I felt somewhat lighter as they sat up, and lighter still when they walked down to the river's edge to dabble their feet in the water. They were gone for a short while, and then they came back laughing, running up the steep bank till they were out of breath. They plopped down on me once again—but only after Olinda scolded Lawrence about drying his feet in the grass before he got close to me. She told him of her promise to her mother and said that she intended to keep it. They sat down toward one edge of me. I supposed that was so their dirty, wet feet wouldn't soil my cloth. After a while, it grew quiet again and I almost wondered if they had fallen asleep. Their hushed whispers let me know that wasn't the case.

Suddenly, a horn blared, and Olinda cried out. Lawrence assured her that the horn was from a tug plodding upriver and she needn't be alarmed. Olinda then said that she could see it now, making its way upriver, although it had been hidden behind the trees earlier.

As it got closer, she said she could see it was pushing a barge full of something covered by a large tarp. Since the river was low, they were just at the right elevation to have a clear view of the boat making its journey north. As the boat churned through the water, the sound it made was not nearly as loud as the blast of its horn. Even so, Olinda sat very still, most likely watching the boat as it headed upriver. Lawrence mentioned that another boat would be passing soon on its way south, because he could see a little farther upriver, and another boat was heading their way.

Lawrence told Olinda that he would get his spyglass from the car so that she could get a better view when she watched the boats. When he returned with it, he taught her how to look through the magnifier. She said she could see very well, that the two boats were much closer to each other now. This is why, Lawrence said, the one boat had sounded its horn to let the other boat know it was approaching. Olinda asked him why the second boat had not responded, but just then there was another blast from the oncoming tugboat.

After the two boats had passed by, Lawrence said it was time to head to his parents' home to visit. They put their shoes back on, and then he and Olinda gathered me up, folded me over, and placed me and the picnic basket in the car again.

As they drove back the short distance to Lawrence's home, he told Olinda a few more things about his family, saying that he was uncertain if he had mentioned them before. He told her that with eight brothers and sisters, he didn't expect her to learn all their names yet, but that in time she would get to know them well. He reminded her that not all of them would be there, because the two oldest were married and no longer lived nearby, and another of his brothers was likely gone with his tug, hauling grain from the local harvests.

Olinda thought this was interesting, and she told Lawrence she had never really given a thought to what happened to the crops her father and brothers harvested at her grandmother's farm. She only knew that they ground some for feed for the animals. It was interesting to know that the rest was most likely hauled by train or barge to places where it was needed.

Lawrence told her that he didn't always transport grain; sometimes rock from the quarry, coal from the nearby mines, or other supplies to many ports along the Mississippi. He said it was a job he loved and hoped to be able to do for a long time. Every port was different, every town along the way had its own uniqueness, and the river was in his blood, since he had grown up right next to it. Then the car stopped, and Lawrence and Olinda got out.

The time passed slowly as I waited for them to return for the drive back to the farm. I thought about all I had experienced today and realized it had been quite an adventure for me. Normally my days were spent listening to the sounds in and around the house at the farm, so today had been quite an unexpected treat. I hoped there would be more of these days to come.

The trip back to the farm after the visit with Lawrence's family passed by so quickly, I barely had time to take in all they were saying to each other. Olinda said that she would indeed have a hard time remembering all the names of his siblings, even with not all of them being present. One of his married brothers and his wife and two children had also been there, so she would have to learn the names of his niece and nephew, too. They made one stop in town—for a drink at Mose's Tavern—before heading to the farm.

As they returned to the car, Olinda mentioned that the day seemed to have gone by so quickly and that she wished for it not to end. Lawrence said he hoped they could spend days like this together more often when he was home, but he likely would be gone the next few days working, and he hoped she understood. Olinda said if that was required for his job, she would have to get used to it. When the car stopped, they hopped out, and Lawrence's strong hands carried me and the basket inside—to what sounded like utter chaos!

It seemed that the time had come for Felicity to deliver her baby. There was such a commotion coming from every room! Doors slammed, and voices intermingled so that I could not tell whose was whose. Lawrence was soon dispatched to call on Doc Bolen, who had come to Parrie just last month to help with old Doc Lemay's practice. Anna had tried to call the doctor on the newly installed telephone, but all the lines were busy and she couldn't get through to the operator.

Lawrence told Olinda that he would go back home after he reached the doctor, so he could be out of the way of everything going on in the house. He told her that he would be in touch with her once he returned from his boat later in the week, but that he would be leaving early the next morning.

When Doc Bolen arrived, he said that Felicity likely would not deliver just yet, so the family all scattered to give the young mother some privacy. I heard Anna, Mary, and Olinda talking as they were sitting in the parlor near me, and from the sound of things, they were each finishing handmade gifts for the new arrival.

Anna said she hoped the afghan she was crocheting would keep her first grandchild warm in the upcoming winter. Mary was apparently working on the final stitches of a knitted bonnet and booties, but her rheumatism was preventing her from staying on task, and she mentioned she would have to stop shortly to let her hands rest awhile. Olinda said she was embroidering a cloth to which she planned to add the newborn's name, once it was known. She planned to stretch it on a frame, and she hoped the stitched sampler would be a nice keepsake for the child.

Near mealtime, the three left the parlor, and I could hear them in the kitchen, preparing supper. Edward and Albert came in from the fields, and Wallace, who had been by Felicity's side, joined them for the meal, too. I heard Wallace ask his mother and grandmother if he should take some food to the young doctor, but just then Doc Bolen called out to say that the time was nearer, and he felt that the baby would arrive shortly.

The family ate their meal in near silence as they awaited any news from the bedroom. Wallace said he was much too nervous to eat and left the table to check on Felicity.

Before long, I heard muffled cries coming from the bedroom—apparently the cries of the new baby, something I had never heard before. I had come into this family when Olinda was a young child, and although I had heard her cry on occasion, it sounded nothing like this. The faint cries grew louder as the nearby bedroom door opened, and Wallace announced that Felicity had delivered a baby boy.

Everyone congratulated him, and I could hear footsteps as people went into the room to see the new addition to the family. There was much laughter and joyous chatter, and soon several passed back through the parlor to give the new mother and baby some time alone. Doc Bolen prepared to leave, turning down Mary and Anna's offer for some supper. He said he had best be on his way.

As the excitement died down that day and the family settled in for the night, I reflected on the events that had unfolded. Most days I witnessed very little, but today had been a momentous one: I had traveled on an outing and was in the home for the birth of a new family member. I was anxious to see what might be lying in wait for me in the days ahead.

Over the next few days, the family was kept quite busy "spoiling," as Mary put it, the new baby, whom they had named Oliver Joseph. Little Ollie, as they took to calling the baby, was quickly becoming the center of attention in the house. Wallace and Felicity had decided to stay in the home for a few weeks, until Felicity was more rested, so that Anna would be able to help her with the baby.

One day, there was a lot of cooking going on, and I heard mention of the word "Thanksgiving" and praising the Lord for all the good things that had come to the family in the past year. I heard them all toasting one another and clinking glasses as they enjoyed a feast at mealtime.

I heard Wallace say that he would start moving some of their belongings back to Edward and Anna's old house in town beginning the next week. Anna asked the couple why they didn't wait until after Christmas, which was only four weeks away. That way they could have a nice celebration before the couple moved on.

Felicity replied that really, there was no hurry, and if Wallace didn't mind the longer commute to the quarry every day, she would enjoy staying a little longer, because she would have very little help once they moved back to town. Other than a few friends and an elderly aunt who had raised her after her parents had died, Felicity would have no one close by to visit and pass her days with while Wallace was at work. It was decided then that Wallace and Felicity would wait until after the New Year to move back to town.

Preparations were now under way in the house for the upcoming Christmas holiday. I could hear the women of the house in the kitchen, busy with baking cookies and fruitcakes. There was much hustling and bustling as they went from room to room, cleaning and rearranging furniture to make room for the tree. I remembered hearing about the tree from past Christmases, and it had played a large role in the festivities.

It wasn't long before Albert came in one day with what he called a fine cedar, cut down from the nearby bluffs. A lot of attention was paid to decorating this tree: They popped popcorn and later gathered together to string the kernels with cranberries and dried orange peels and cinnamon sticks to make a garland for the tree.

Anna came into the room, saying that she had the box with ornaments for decorating the tree, and then I heard the others rummaging through the box. They talked and laughed as they hung the ornaments on the tree, exclaiming about certain ones they remembered from their childhood, as well as new ones they had made this year for young Ollie.

Mary brought out her own box of decorations, including a star to place on top of the tree. I heard Ollie crying, and he must have been hungry, because Felicity left the room, saying she would nurse him and return shortly to help them finish up. Wallace announced that even though Ollie wasn't yet old enough to join in on the decorating, he would hold Oliver up to the tree as he placed the star at the very top, continuing the tradition that had been passed down through generations—the youngest family member has the honor of placing the star. Although little Ollie wouldn't be able to hold it in his hands, he could participate in his own way.

After the family attended mass on Christmas morning, Lawrence came back to the house with them to visit Olinda and share Christmas dinner with the family. They all sat in the dining room near the parlor, and I could hear them talking about the fine meal of chicken and dumplings the women had prepared.

Mary said that her mother had prepared this dish every Christmas, and she had loved it as a child. She seemed happy to pass this tradition on to Anna and Olinda. Lawrence said it was one of the best meals he had ever had, and he hoped that Olinda would learn how to cook them herself so she could make them for him often. When Edward asked him what he meant by this, Lawrence gave a vague response.

After the family had finished their meal, they came back into the parlor to exchange Christmas gifts. They were all laughing and talking as they opened each one. It seemed that little Ollie was the recipient of most of the gifts—small trinkets and toys, handmade clothing, and a rocking horse that Wallace had made for him to ride when he was a little older.

As everyone was clearing up the wrappings and trimmings, Anna exclaimed that Lawrence hadn't given Olinda a gift yet. Olinda had given Lawrence a beautiful pocket watch earlier, but it had gone unnoticed at the time that Lawrence had no gift for her.

At that moment, I—along with everyone in the room—heard Lawrence say that he did have a gift for Olinda. Before anyone could look for an unwrapped gift, he announced that he very much wished for Olinda's hand in marriage. Olinda gasped with excitement! Then Lawrence apparently produced a lovely engagement ring for Olinda. I heard everyone's excited congratulations and the sound of the other men slapping Lawrence on the back and tearful exclamations from Olinda and Anna.

In the background, young Ollie must have been scared by all the excitement, for he started in with a high-pitched howling. Everyone laughed about that. I heard Felicity comforting him and telling him that this was a happy time, and they were sorry to have made so much noise and frightened him.

Edward announced that the news deserved a toast, so he brought in a bottle of his homemade wine and enough glasses so that all could share not only a Christmas drink, but also a celebration for the newly engaged couple.

Later, I overheard Olinda and Anna already making wedding plans, while Lawrence and the men played cards at a table in the corner of the parlor. Felicity and Mary sat nearby playing with Ollie, who was rattling a new toy he had received as one of his gifts.

The day ended with a light supper of leftovers from dinner, and more wine, eggnog, cookies, and fruitcake. Later, when Lawrence announced it was time for him to leave, Olinda accompanied him out to the porch so they could say their goodbyes.

Once the couple went outside, Edward asked Anna if she was as happy as he was that Lawrence had asked Olinda to be his bride. She responded that she was, very much so. She agreed with Edward that Lawrence would make a fine husband for their only daughter, and she hoped that they would have many happy years together.

Anna went on to say that Olinda and Lawrence were probably at this very moment out on the porch deciding when the wedding would take place. She commented that because there would be much to do to prepare for the wedding, she hoped it wouldn't be too soon—they needed time to sew her a lovely wedding dress.

When Olinda came back inside after Lawrence had left, Mary told Olinda that she had something she wanted to give her. She told Olinda that she would love it if Olinda would wear the wedding dress that Mary had worn when she married Olinda's grandfather, Joseph. Mary mentioned that Anna had also worn the dress when she married Edward, so it would be fitting if Olinda wished to wear it, too.

Olinda was overjoyed with the prospect and said she hoped it would fit. Anna exclaimed that she thought it a lovely idea and now they would not have to sew a new one. Then she remembered that Mary had given the dress to her cousin Sarah for her wedding several years ago, and it had not been returned. When Anna reminded Mary of this, Mary replied that the dress had indeed been returned, and that it was stored away in the attic. She said Edward could bring it down the next day, and they could inspect it to see if it needed repairs of any kind or perhaps alterations to the style.

Edward asked Olinda if a date had been set, and she said that they would have to talk with Father Duquette, but that they hoped to be married sometime in April. Anna said that would give them just enough time to make the plans for a church wedding and reserve the church basement for the reception for friends and family.

Olinda said they were afraid that the reception room in the church basement wouldn't be nearly big enough, since Lawrence came from such a large family. If they agreed, she said, she and Lawrence thought maybe they could host the reception in the barn. Edward said it would take a lot of cleaning and shuffling of implements and farm equipment, but it could be done if that is what they wished. Talk soon turned to all they would have to do to have the wedding reception at the farm.

As I listened to their lively conversation about all the wedding plans, I realized just how much I cared for all of them. For it was just then that I understood that this young couple would be a new branch of my family. I wondered where Olinda and Lawrence would make their home, and I thought about the fact that in just a few short months, I would have new surroundings again.

The plans for Olinda and Lawrence's wedding were moving along quickly, and by New Year's Eve, a date had been chosen. Easter that year would be on April 4th, which would bring Lent to a close, so everyone agreed on April 10th as the date for the wedding. When the family had a midnight toast to the New Year of 1926, it was with great hope that the year ahead would be a prosperous and healthy one for all.

Shortly after the new year began, Wallace, Felicity, and Ollie moved into their new home in town—the former home of Edward and Anna. Mary's house seemed so much more quiet after they had gone. Everyone missed all the noise and activity of having young Ollie around.

Anna, Olinda, and Mary examined the wedding dress and soon decided that it would be much simpler to use parts of the old dress with some newer fabric, because much of the cloth on the dress had deteriorated over the years. In addition, Anna's cousin, who had borrowed the dress and returned it some ten years ago, had failed to mention that the dress had been badly torn. Some of the best trims, pearl buttons, and ribbons were snipped off, and a newer dress was designed.

The women spent their spare time that winter sewing the new dress and making lists of food they would need to prepare for the reception. Since the wedding would be so early in the spring, Olinda decided that she would use daffodils, hyacinths, and narcissus from Mary's garden in her bouquet and Lawrence's boutonniere. Olinda had already spoken to Minnie, who had been married two years before, to see if she would stand up for her as matron of honor, and Minnie had agreed. Lawrence had asked his oldest brother, Armand, to be his best man.

The day of the ceremony was a bright, sunny day, and unseasonably warm. Olinda was overjoyed that the flowers she had anticipated using from Mary's garden were already blooming in abundance, and the bouquet she made that morning was practically overflowing with beautiful flowers.

The barn had been cleaned and decorated. All of its inhabitants—the two work horses and the three dairy cows—had been taken to neighboring farms over the past few days while all the preparations were being made. Sprigs of more blooms were arranged in jars and vases and placed on the tables.

I even got to play a small part, not in the ceremony, but at the reception. Olinda and Anna had strung a rope from one end of the horse stalls to the other and hung blankets and quilts along it to hide the unsightly area. I was chosen to be at the center of the line, behind the head table where the wedding couple, their attendants, and parents were to sit.

The rest of the barn was set up with tables and chairs borrowed from neighbors and friends in order to accommodate all the guests, with a small area left bare for dancing. In all, more than 100 people had been invited, and nearly all of them were able to attend.

After the ceremony at St. Joseph's, everyone came to the barn for the celebration. I heard everyone exclaiming how beautiful Olinda looked in her lovely dress and how delicious the food was. The food had been prepared that morning and the day before, and it was set out once the guests had all arrived. Following the meal, there was a lovely cake, so I heard, and homemade wine and lemonade to toast the new couple.

Several of Lawrence's brothers were musicians, and they played music on their squeezebox, fiddle, and harmonicas. The music and dancing, laughter and conversation, went on throughout the afternoon and into the evening. It sounded like everyone was having a wonderful time! The celebration ended all too soon, and I felt strong arms lifting me off the rope and folding me over. Lawrence said to Olinda that tonight they would be nice and warm with this wedding gift from her parents, since the air had turned quite chilly as the sun had set.

As Olinda and Lawrence left the barn, the guests ushered them to the door and showered them with handfuls of rice—a tradition to wish the couple prosperity and fertility in their new union. When they reached their new home, which turned out to be the former home of Mrs. Tarantina, they unfolded me onto the bed, and more rice sprinkled onto the floor. They laughed at this, saying they should indeed have good luck, because the rice had blessed their new home as well. From that night on, I fulfilled the purpose for which I was intended, as a wedding quilt for Olinda and her husband.

9

My life in the home of Olinda and Lawrence was very much what it had been in Anna and Edward's home. Olinda, now a married woman, was not expected to continue working at her old job in the dress factory. Lawrence had told her that he would provide for her and any children they might have in the future, so she carried out the daily chores of cleaning, cooking, and sewing—all the things I had become accustomed to with Anna.

Lawrence's family had given the young couple a radio as a wedding gift, and Olinda frequently played it during the day. It seemed to keep her company while Lawrence was away on the river, and she sang along or hummed while she worked. The sound from this contraption was not unlike that of Anna's phonograph, yet I marveled at the music and voices I heard coming across the sound waves. I often had trouble knowing if there were visitors in the house or if what I heard came from the wireless.

Since Mrs. Tarantina had never taken advantage of the telephone system, Lawrence and Olinda had one installed in their new home. Olinda rarely used it except to speak to Anna or Minnie, and most times when she wanted to make a call, the operator would tell her that the lines were all full and she would have to wait her turn.

Lawrence was gone with his boat for days at a time, and then he would be back home for several days before leaving again. He and Olinda fell into a pattern that seemed to work well for them.

When Edward had business in town, he and Anna often came to visit their daughter when Lawrence was on the river, to check in on her or keep her company. Anna loved to spend time in Evangeline's old house, and I was overjoyed to hear her voice. I was surprised by how much I had missed her, and I looked forward to her visits with Olinda probably almost as much as Olinda did herself.

When Lawrence was home, he and Olinda occasionally entertained their families or a few young couples who were very good friends. They seemed to enjoy all these visits; sometimes they left the house for outings as well. Edward and Anna were invited to Sunday dinner now and then, and sometimes Lawrence's family came to visit, too.

With Wallace and Felicity living next door, the two women often walked across their yards to visit, much like Anna and Evangeline had done. Felicity would always have young Ollie in tow. He was beginning to babble and crawl, and he seemed to keep her quite occupied.

Wallace and Lawrence got along well, too, but both were hardworking men who kept busy with their jobs. They didn't seem to socialize much on their own, only when the couples were together, and I seldom heard them discussing anything other than fishing, hunting, or their work—but those things didn't interest me at all.

Albert had begun working as a carpenter after his father took over the farm. He still helped out there occasionally, but he wasn't needed at the farm nearly as much since Edward had hired a young farmhand. Now and then, Albert would stop by to have supper with Olinda, either when she was alone or sometimes when Lawrence was home, too.

Albert would tell Olinda about all the things he was learning in his new trade. He was specializing in cabinetmaking, and he seemed to enjoy it immensely. Albert shared that he was interested in taking over the shop in town once the owner was ready to retire and sell the business, which is where Albert now resided—in the living quarters above the shop. Olinda seemed to look forward to Albert's visits, and she told him to come back soon nearly every time he left. During her nightly prayers, I sometimes heard her ask for help in finding a woman to share Albert's solitary life. Although he didn't seem lonely, she felt he would be much happier if he could settle down with a family of his own.

The warm spring days turned into a hot summer. Olinda would sometimes be gone during the day so much that I would get quite lonely. I found out, when Lawrence came home from one of his trips, just where she had been. He asked if she had been keeping busy, and she told him that she had been spending a lot of time at Minnie's, now that Minnie was expecting another baby. Olinda had offered to help out, because Minnie had been instructed by the doctor to stay in bed. She had already lost two babies since her marriage two years ago.

Olinda, Minnie's mother, Adele, and several young women from church were all taking turns helping with laundry, cleaning, and cooking meals for Minnie and her husband George. Helping her friend and trying to keep up with her own gardening and housework were keeping Olinda quite busy. She offered that at least all the activity made the time pass quickly until Lawrence was home again.

Soon the crispness of autumn air arrived. The seasons seemed to change so quickly that I could hardly keep up. I knew they were changing, because I could feel the difference in the air in the house, and because of the conversations I overheard.

Early one morning, I heard Anna's voice when she and Edward came to visit Olinda. It sounded as though Anna was crying. From what I could understand, Mary had passed away during the night. Anna said she didn't use the telephone to share this sad news, because she and Edward were already coming into town, and she wanted to break the news to Olinda in person. A heart attack, Anna said, had claimed her mother just like it had taken Mary's mother years ago.

Anna went on to say that it had been less than a year since she had lost her dear friend Evangeline, and that Mary's death felt much, much worse. Anna added that she didn't know how she would be able to deal with the loss of two of the most important women in her life. Olinda and Anna both sobbed and tried to console one another. I could hear Edward trying to ease their pain, but he finally must have decided to let them cry it out. He quietly slipped out the back door to give them time to grieve.

As was their custom in times of sorrow, the two women took out their rosaries. They prayed for Mary to rest in peace. Later, when Edward came back into the house, he and Anna left to go speak with Father Duquette about planning Mary's funeral. The undertaker, new to the town, had already been to the farm to transport Mary's body to the funeral home, which had opened just recently. The town of Parrie was beginning to grow, and with this added service, loved ones who had passed on need not be laid out in their own homes as in the past.

Mary's funeral was held on a cold day, which also happened to be All Souls Day—November 2, 1926.

The air had a sharp bite to it, so much so that Olinda took me off the bed to accompany them in the car for warmth. Lawrence had been working on the car's heater, but apparently it was still not working properly. He had to stop several times on the way to the church and the cemetery to scrape frost off the windshield.

I tried my best to keep them comfortable, but Olinda exclaimed after returning home from the funeral that she could not seem to get warm. Lawrence took me into the house and bundled me around Olinda's body to warm her as he stoked the coals in the grate of the heating stove. Olinda remarked that he was such a good husband and he took such wonderful care of her, especially now that she was in her condition. I wondered what that meant, and was soon to find out.

One afternoon, a few weeks after Mary's funeral, Anna and Edward came to visit Olinda and Lawrence. Olinda told them that Minnie had delivered her baby the previous night. She and George had a beautiful little girl they had named Josephine Marie, and both mother and baby were doing fine.

Anna said that she was so very happy for them, after the two previous losses they had endured. She went on to say that now Olinda wouldn't have to spend quite as much time over there helping out. Olinda told her parents that it was probably a good idea that she would not have all the extra work of another household to care for. Then she told them that she and Lawrence had an announcement of their own to share.

Anna guessed the news before the words were out! It seemed that a new arrival was going to take place in their home as well. Olinda was expecting a baby!

Anna and Edward excitedly congratulated the couple. From my spot on the bed in the next room, I could hear all the shouts of congratulations and laughing. This news excited me, too, for I had become accustomed to noisier surroundings in their other homes where there were children around. I had loved to hear young Ollie's squeals and coos every day, and I was overjoyed at the thought of experiencing this again on a daily basis with Lawrence and Olinda's new baby.

Anna told Olinda how overjoyed she was that this news came so soon after Mary's death. She said that when one life is gone, another one takes its place, and it seemed fitting that Olinda should now be carrying a child. Her only regret was that Mary would not be here to see the new arrival. She would have so loved to witness the birth of a new family member.

Anna asked Olinda when she thought the baby might arrive, and Olinda said probably sometime in May, from her best calculations. Anna mentioned that it would be nice if the baby was born on Mother's Day—what a splendid gift that would be!

Olinda wasted no time converting the empty spare room into a nursery. Anna visited one day and helped her clean it and hang new wallpaper. Evangeline would have been overjoyed at the thought of a baby in her old house, Anna said. Olinda agreed, and she said that she had felt blessed since the day they walked into the home, almost as if Evangeline was there with them, looking out for their well-being.

After the walls were finished, Edward came and brought the old crib, which hadn't been used since Olinda herself was a baby, except for the short time when Ollie had slept in it while living at their home. They took some time deciding where to place it in the room, along with a small dresser and one of Mary's old rocking chairs. Olinda exclaimed that she couldn't wait for Lawrence to return and see everything they had done.

Olinda had a pot of soup cooking on the stove that day, and she invited Anna and Edward to stay for supper. When Lawrence came home shortly afterward and they had shown him the room, he said he thought this would be the luckiest baby in the world, having such a fine place to lay its head at night.

After they had eaten supper, they headed into the parlor to listen to the news on the radio. The news announcer was reporting about the devastation in

Arkansas and parts of Missouri the previous weekend, when several tornadoes had swept through that area. More than 70 people had been killed or were still listed as missing in the aftermath.

Edward reminded Anna and Olinda of the time when the children were young that a twister had formed near Parrie and they had all gone to the cellar. Anna said she remembered it very well, because that was the day she had just finished the quilt that was now lying on Olinda and Lawrence's bed. Olinda said she must have only been about eight years old or so, but that she remembered that day as well. She even remembered that after the storm had passed, she had picked up peaches that had been knocked off the trees. They all agreed that they had been very lucky. There were no injuries as a result of the Parrie twister.

That night, as Olinda and Lawrence slept beneath me, I recalled the events of the day. My, oh my, they all remembered the day of the terrible storm, just as I did. I remembered that I had felt very special to be taken down to the cellar with them. So much had changed over the years! Here was Olinda, now starting a family of her own. Normally, I only thought of the passage of time by noting the day that events took place. Now their conversation had me thinking back and reminiscing about all I had been through in the past many years with them. I wondered if someday in the future I would look back on these days, too.

IO

Mother's Day was fast approaching and—as Anna had predicted—Olinda was due to have her baby any day. Lawrence took time off from his boat runs so he would be home when the time came. While he was home, he also seemed to be taking over most of the household chores. He did the cooking and cleaning and anything else that needed to be done.

Lawrence kept Olinda as comfortable as he could, propping her up with pillows and helping her to the table for meals. She told him all the fuss was not necessary, but he insisted, so she let him indulge her. He asked Felicity—and Ollie, of course—to come over and spend time with Olinda anytime he left the house for errands around town.

Anna stopped by quite often too, and coddled Olinda like a mother hen with her chick. She was so excited for her daughter to deliver that she brought the baby's gift early.

Anna had been spending time making a tiny version of me—a baby quilt, she called it. From what I heard, it was not made from nearly the amount of special scraps that I was, but from whatever Anna had on hand. Since it was smaller, I got the impression that it hadn't taken her as much time to complete it either. I heard Anna say it was a tied quilt, one that she had made by tying pieces of yarn to hold it together rather than stitching with thread. She said that she had been so busy with new calves and chicks and other responsibilities at the farm that she didn't see how she could have finished a traditional quilt before the baby's arrival. Nevertheless, it must have been beautiful, and Olinda thanked Anna for it over and over again.

Sunday, May 8, 1927, turned out to be a momentous date. I had a hunch something was going on, because of all the commotion when Lawrence and Olinda awoke that day. Olinda carried on for some time, and Lawrence scurried about getting dressed, bumping into things, and running to telephone the doctor. It appeared that the time had come for the baby to arrive! And Anna had been right—it was also Mother's Day.

Olinda advised Lawrence to tell the doctor to hurry, because she had a feeling it wouldn't be long. Her pains were coming very hard and fast, without any previous warning. Lawrence said the operator told him she would ring Doc Bolen right away.

About that time, Wallace and Felicity and baby Ollie stopped by before first mass to drop off cinnamon rolls fresh from Felicity's oven. When she heard that Olinda was in labor, Felicity wanted to stay, but Lawrence said that Olinda would probably much rather have as few people as possible around for the birth. He did ask Felicity to give Anna a call to let her know that Olinda was in labor.

Just as the family was taking their leave, after Felicity had called Anna to let her know that Olinda's time had come, Doc Bolen arrived. Events moved rather quickly then, much faster than I remembered when Ollie was born. This time I was much closer to the action, right on the bed with Olinda!

That didn't last long though—I soon felt myself being lifted up and tossed across the room to the floor. The wooden floor felt cool and smooth to me, and I marveled at this new sensation. I can't say that I minded, because I was a bit wary about what was taking place on the bed. I appreciated the detachment of being an observer rather than a participant, and I waited patiently for good news.

Doc Bolen asked Lawrence to first bring more pillows, so he could prop Olinda up, and then to make sure they had plenty of towels and a pan of warm water for bathing the baby once it arrived. There was a lot of commotion, and I was glad to be out of harm's way.

Soon Lawrence returned with everything Doc Bolen had asked for. When after a very short time Olinda's cries grew louder, Doc Bolen asked Lawrence to step out of the room. Lawrence insisted that he wanted to stay. The young doctor cautioned him that he was not going to be responsible if Lawrence felt ill or fainted, but Lawrence replied that he wasn't leaving her side.

The doctor then announced that Olinda was progressing much more quickly than he had anticipated and that the baby would be born very soon. Olinda was making grunting and panting noises, the like of which I had never heard before. I felt so bad for her, knowing that this must be such an ordeal, but hopefully it was one that would end soon—and happily.

Before long, there was a clattering coming from outside the house: Edward had driven Anna into town as quickly as he could. Lawrence left the room to let them in, exclaiming that they must have literally flown to have arrived so quickly. Edward chuckled in response, and then immediately excused himself and said that he would wait for any news over at Wallace and Felicity's house.

Early in Olinda's pregnancy, I remembered hearing her tell Anna that she hoped to have her mother in attendance when the time came to deliver their little bundle, but that she didn't want to have quite the audience that Felicity had endured when Ollie was born. Edward must have remembered Anna telling him this, because he appeared to have honored his daughter's wishes.

Lawrence hurried back to Olinda's side, and Anna had barely set foot in the room when Olinda gave one more anguished heave and I heard the first feeble whimpers of the newborn—a girl, the doctor said.

Doc Bolen exclaimed that Olinda had had one of the quickest deliveries he had ever witnessed. He checked the baby over, and after announcing that she was fit and healthy, he proceeded to tend to Olinda. Then he asked Anna if she wished to give her granddaughter her first bath. Lawrence declared that he was just so happy that they both were doing well, no matter how fast it had taken place.

The infant gave a lusty cry as she was being bathed, and Lawrence gratefully murmured his thanks to Doc Bolen for getting there in time. After Doc Bolen had helped Olinda settle in, he gave her a few pointers on breastfeeding and a bottle of pills to ease any discomfort. He then asked the new parents to sign the birth certificate, adding the name they had chosen: Grace Evangeline. Once that was done, he took his leave, wished them well, and told Lawrence to keep him informed of their condition and to call if they needed him for any reason.

When Anna had finished bathing the baby, she wrapped her in the new quilt and handed her to the young couple. They marveled aloud at the exquisiteness of their new offspring. Anna was overjoyed with

the name they had chosen: Grace was her grandmother's name, and Evangeline had been her dearest
friend. Olinda said she loved both names and that
Lawrence had picked the boy's name, but they would
just save it and hope for a boy next time.

Anna then gathered me up from the floor and
smoothed and tucked me around the new family. She
said that she would be leaving them soon so that
she and Edward could attend late mass, and that she
would pray for blessings for the family. She added that
she and Edward would return later to check in on
them.

Anna brewed coffee while she tidied up. She gathered laundry to take home with her and told them
that she could at least relieve Lawrence of that burden. Before they left, she brought in a tray with coffee
and the rolls Felicity had made for them. She told
Lawrence that in her hurry to get there quickly, she
had left something at home—the hen she had butch-
ered the previous day with the intention of cooking
them some soup. He replied that there was plenty for
them to eat and that she needn't worry, because he
had been preparing food for the two of them for several days now.

With Olinda and the baby resting in the bed, and
Lawrence beside her, Anna said it looked as if they
had all they needed in the world right there in that
room.

As for myself, I felt the most incredible feeling of contentment at that very moment. I was experiencing things in a much more intimate way than ever before in all my 15 years with the family. I tried to figure out what this meant, but I came to the conclusion that it meant something much deeper than anything I could understand.

II

If ever there was a more delightful child than Gracie, as everyone called her, I would be hard pressed to find one. She was the apple of her daddy's eye, and her mommy's pride and joy.

I don't say that just because she was the first child born into the family I had come to know and love, because there had also been young Ollie, who was now growing into a sturdy, boisterous boy. Little Josie, Minnie and George's daughter just a few months older than Gracie, would come to visit with her mother, and she seemed like a sweet child, too. But Gracie—she was something special.

From the day she was born, I had felt such affection for her. I couldn't quite figure out what was so unique about our relationship, but it gave me something to think about as she grew day by day. I don't mean to imply that Gracie was perfect, because no child is. As a matter of fact, she indirectly caused my baptism.

Over the years, I had heard the family talk about taking baths to cleanse their bodies, and I always knew that Anna and Olinda laundered clothing, sheets, towels, and what not. However, during my existence, it had never happened to me.

It wasn't that they didn't keep me clean, but most times I was taken outside to air out, and sometimes I was beaten with something hard or was shaken out. Then I was brought back in and placed on the quilt rack, in a chifforobe, or—since Lawrence and Olinda's wedding—on the bed. A few times, Olinda had taken a rag or cloth to a certain spot on my form to scrub out whatever might have marked me, but for the most part, I was kept nice and dry. Since I wasn't really used until after the wedding, there had been no need for a real washing.

When Anna had finished me, she had told Olinda that the more you laundered a quilt, the quicker it would deteriorate, and so to do so sparingly. Olinda had told Lawrence she thought this was an old wives' tale—one that had been passed down through the years when women didn't have the time or means to clean such a large item. Still, she had taken Anna's advice. After almost three years of everyday use, however, I was about to have my day in the bath, and the cause of this was something I never would have suspected.

Olinda, although not working a regular job outside the home, had been commissioned by several well-to-do ladies of Parrie to sew dresses for them and their daughters. Nearly every afternoon, she spent her free time sewing while Gracie napped, and often later in the evening, too, when the toddler had been put to bed. Her services were much sought after, it seemed, for she was quite the seamstress. She had learned much from Anna, as well as from her job in the dress factory, where she had often been highly praised for her work.

I heard Olinda mention to Lawrence how lucky they were that she was able to stay home with Gracie and contribute to the family income in that way. As word spread about Olinda's sewing skills, she often got orders to make curtains and quilt tops or do alterations, in addition to sewing new garments.

One day, Olinda was sewing at her machine in the corner of the bedroom. Gracie, who had just finished her lunch of a jelly bread sandwich, was playing nearby. Olinda was in a hurry to finish this particular commissioned piece—new altar cloths to be used at the upcoming anniversary mass at church. She was trying to complete them and had occupied Gracie with some toys.

After a time, Gracie must have grown bored and wandered out of the room to explore. Olinda was focused on her sewing and didn't realize that Gracie was gone. She soon saw what a mistake she had made: She turned around to see Gracie sitting on top of me, smearing my surface with jelly straight from the jar that had been left on the kitchen table. Olinda shrieked and picked Gracie up, scolding her, but the damage had been done. This was the strangest sensation I had ever experienced! The wet stickiness of the jelly was such a contrast to my normal warm and dry self.

Before I knew quite what had happened, I heard Olinda preparing a bath for Gracie. Shortly after that, Gracie was put in her crib for a nap.

As for me, Olinda rolled me up off the bed and tossed me into a tub of warm, sudsy water for my own bath. Oh my, what a wonderful experience! This felt much like when I had been placed on the clothesline—a floating sensation, but something entirely different, too, with my first experience of having so much water around me.

My fibers lifted and swayed as Olinda scrubbed away, releasing all the sticky jelly that was stuck on my form. She left me to sit in the bubbly water while she completed other tasks. Finally, she returned to rinse and wring me out. That was another strange experience! All that twisting and pulling—I felt as though I might be torn in two! Soon, after nearly having the life squeezed out of me, I was hanging in the sunshine and flapping in the warm summer breeze as if I had not a care in the world.

It was at that moment that I realized something was different. I felt saggy and flatter, not my usual fluffy self. I wondered if Anna had been right when she said that washing a quilt too much might make it wear out sooner. Oh, I prayed that was not the case! As the day wore on, with the warm breeze in the air, I felt myself getting back to normal. After a while, Olinda came to retrieve me, and she placed me back on the bed. I could tell that I was on top of clean sheets, which she must have decided to launder, too. I had the sensation of being brand new—fluffy once again—and I realized that this bath had revitalized me more than I could have imagined. I reassured myself that I was as useful as ever, and I looked forward to another such experience in the future.

That evening when Lawrence came home, Olinda told him about the jelly incident. He and Olinda had a good laugh, but at the time it happened I don't think Olinda thought it was very funny. Lawrence said if that was the only mischief Gracie got herself into in her lifetime, they would be lucky!

From that day on, Olinda took more care to ensure that Gracie was well occupied while she sewed. When Lawrence was home from boat runs, he offered to take the child for walks or outside to play in the yard. He often let her accompany him when he visited his parents or ran errands in town. That helped Olinda get caught up with her sewing orders, and then the family could enjoy quiet evenings together, playing with Gracie and listening to the radio.

That summer was a particularly steamy one, and on many nights, I felt myself pushed to the very end of the bed as the couple would lie with only the sheet on them or even no covering at all. The oppressive heat must have affected Gracie as well, for she was cranky and stubborn. I heard Lawrence and Olinda refer to her as being in the terrible two's, a term I had also heard Felicity use to describe Ollie when he was that age.

Anna and Edward stopped by one day, and it was during this visit that I learned that Olinda was expecting a second child. Anna and Edward were pleased for the young couple and mentioned how much they hoped that Gracie would get a little brother. Olinda and Lawrence said they didn't care one way or the other what the new baby would be, just as long as it was healthy like Gracie. They said that this baby would be arriving sometime the following March, so the two children would be nearly three years apart. Olinda mentioned that she was happy that Gracie would be a little more grown up by then and would hopefully be a helpful big sister.

Edward and Lawrence talked about the falling grain prices and Lawrence's boat runs, which had been noticeably dwindling.

Edward said that Albert was lucky to have just completed a big job for a new church in St. Louis. He had been commissioned to build an altar, communion rail, and 44 church pews. He had had to hire two helpers in order to complete the job on time, but they had been able to finish on schedule and had just been paid for the work. Albert had made quite a bit of money on this particular contract, enough to purchase more raw lumber. He wanted to work on smaller items to sell in his shop. He hoped to be able to produce items that people would need, because it often seemed that the things people wanted were just beyond their grasp.

They also talked about Wallace, who was still working at the quarry and had worked up to being foreman. As times were getting tougher, Wallace was worried that they would have to let some of the workers go.

There were more and more ominous signs that something was changing in the town of Parrie and beyond, but no one could predict the hard times that were ahead. Many years later, I would look back on this time in moments of solitude and remember all that had happened and how it had affected everyone I had come to know. For now, the family could only brace themselves for what everyone would eventually refer to as The Great Depression.

12

· 1930 ·

The new year brought hardship and sacrifice for Lawrence and Olinda. There were growing concerns over how they could stretch Lawrence's dwindling paychecks and still provide for another mouth to feed in the household. The loss of almost half of his boat runs affected them more than they could have imagined.

They talked about how the previous autumn's financial crash on Wall Street in New York had signaled the beginning of something no one had seen coming. Its results had begun to filter down to small town America, and many were beginning to feel the effects.

Olinda had very few sewing jobs. Everyone in Parrie and the neighboring towns was holding onto their money to pay for food on their tables and coal in their stoves—and the latter was beginning to become scarce. Because farmers were more self-sufficient and less reliant on outside forces, Anna and Edward were able to share a lot of food from the farm with their children. On one of Anna's visits to bring Olinda fresh eggs and milk, she said that she and

Edward would do everything in their power to help them.

Looking back, I don't know how Lawrence and Olinda would have survived had it not been for the help from her parents. Lawrence's parents, who were more elderly and less well off than Anna and Edward, were in no position to assist them.

Lawrence's mother, Marie, had serious health problems, and she had gone to live in St. Louis, where she could be cared for by one of Lawrence's sisters, who lived there with her husband and children. Marie later turned gravely ill and was taken to a hospital. She was placed on an iron lung machine to help with chronic respiratory problems that were the result of having polio as a child. Lawrence's father, Emile, was still living near the river with Lawrence's youngest brother, Michael, who helped his father by taking care of their small farm and lighting Emile's fires along the river when needed.

The treatment Marie received could not cure her advanced disease. She succumbed to her illness and passed away near the end of January that year. Her body was brought back to Parrie for a funeral and burial, and the young couple experienced yet another loss of a family member.

Lawrence took the news of his mother's death particularly hard. I often heard him and Olinda arguing about the state of their financial affairs, with her saying that he needed to pull out of his depression and find some sort of work. It had been weeks since he had had any transports with his boat, and she worried about the strain on their household.

Then Edward asked Lawrence to work for him. Edward's farmhand had up and left after the first of the year, moving to Arkansas to be nearer his family. Edward added that whenever Lawrence had the opportunity to go out in his boat, he could have the time away. Lawrence balked at first, not wanting to step away from what he enjoyed so much. However, he realized that although he loved the river and his boat, he could do nothing to change the fact that life as they knew it had changed. He was no stranger to farm work, after all, having helped his father, although that was on a much smaller scale than Edward would require. That winter, it was the farm work, along with a few short runs with his tugboat, that kept them solvent.

By this time, Olinda was less than two months away from delivering the new baby. I heard Doc Bolen tell her, when he stopped by one day, that with the opening of the new hospital in Robertsville just 7 miles away, he felt it best that she go there to deliver. He said that his practice was stretched so thin and covered so much area, ever since old Doc Lemay had stopped practicing after his stroke, that he didn't know if he would be available for her when the time came. He remembered her quick delivery of Gracie and said that if he was out of town on a call, she would not have anyone to assist her.

Doc Bolen said that he was in the process of getting another physician to help him, but that the new recruit would not be arriving until late May. Robertsville Hospital had several physicians who were capable of delivering the baby, he said. Olinda agreed, but she expressed her concerns about the added costs of a hospital birth. Doc Bolen assured her that it was not as expensive as she might think, and that being in the hospital setting would allow her to get some much needed rest. He added that the hospital took charity cases and even installment payments if the patient was experiencing undue hardship.

As the time grew near for Olinda to deliver, she also worried about getting to the hospital. Late one night she and Lawrence devised a plan to ask Felicity and Wallace to care for Gracie; she would call Lawrence at the farm or ring Albert at his nearby shop to drive her to Robertsville. As it turned out, neither plan was needed.

Olinda awoke one morning after a very restless night. As Lawrence prepared to leave for the farm, she suggested that he should wear something nicer than his work clothing, because she felt it was time to go to the hospital. He dressed quickly and called Felicity. As Lawrence helped Olinda into the car to take her to the hospital, Felicity came over to get Gracie. I heard doors slam and the car's engine start up, and they quickly drove away.

The house was unusually quiet. Although Lawrence returned later that night, no one else was at home with him, and I did not hear him speak on the telephone to anyone. He would leave each morning and come back late into the night, and it was several days before I knew the outcome of the baby's birth.

When the family returned home, I found out that they had a new baby boy. His name was James Emile, Olinda told Gracie when she introduced her to her new brother. Olinda must have really missed Gracie while she was away from her, because I heard her exclaiming how much bigger Gracie looked as she planted noisy kisses on the toddler. I wondered how much Gracie could have grown in those few days, but soon I realized that Olinda probably meant that Gracie seemed bigger when compared to the baby.

James was a fussy baby who suffered from colic almost from the very beginning. He was awake and crying most of the night, so that Olinda was awake into the wee hours, and then he slept much of the day. I worried that Olinda was not getting any rest, with the baby keeping her awake at nighttime and Gracie needing to be cared for during the day. Olinda could not even take a nap! Anna offered advice, mostly old-time interventions that failed to produce results.

One day, Anna came to check on the young family and to help with some of the household chores. She ordered Olinda to lie down for a nap while she watched the children, folded the laundry, and made supper for the family. Anna offered to take Gracie home with her when she left that day, but Olinda refused. She said that Gracie had never spent the night away from home before, and she worried that Gracie might miss her mommy, or that she might cry and want to go home in the middle of the night if she woke up in strange surroundings. Surely, she told Anna, James would settle into a routine soon.

Olinda stubbornly told Anna that she didn't want to admit to failure in her efforts to be a good mother to both of her children. Anna assured her that she didn't see it as an admission of defeat, but rather as providing respite for Olinda from an exhausting situation. But Olinda held her ground, and Gracie stayed at home—for the time being.

A few days later, Felicity dropped by with a pot of stew for Olinda's family, and she saw for herself just how worn out Olinda seemed to be. She offered to help with the laundry and cleaning, but young Ollie was a boisterous little boy, and the noise he made put Olinda even more on edge. Olinda was relieved though, when Felicity offered to take Gracie to her house to play so that Olinda could lie down while James took his usual long daytime nap.

Lawrence did all he could for her when he was at home, watching Gracie so Olinda could sleep during the day, but on days he went to work, his hands were tied. At night, when she got up with James, she always reminded Lawrence that he needed his sleep for work the next day.

As the days wore on, it became apparent that something needed to change: Olinda was nearly at her wit's end. Because she couldn't get enough sleep, she became upset easily, and she cried for no apparent reason. Finally, having exhausted all her home remedies, she called Doc Bolen, who came for a visit. He prescribed a tonic for James, but he told her that it would take several days to begin working. Doc Bolen advised Olinda to try to eat sensibly and drink a lot of fluids to keep her strength up.

This proved to be harder than expected, and one evening she nearly fell asleep during dinner, which consisted of little more than boiled eggs and some sliced bread with butter and jelly. Lawrence told her that she couldn't go on this way, because she was getting much too thin and was wearing herself down to nothing. Olinda said she really only wanted to sleep.

The next day, Anna came into town to help Olinda again. She repeated her offer to have Gracie come to the farm, saying that it would be no trouble for her at all, and that Gracie would enjoy the change. Still, Olinda felt that she could—and should—manage on her own, now that James had the medicine prescribed by Doc Bolen. So at the end of the day, Anna went home by herself.

Finally, after a particularly grueling night, Lawrence could take no more. He said that he was going to take Gracie to the farm with him that morning to give Olinda some rest. By this point, a tearful Olinda was truly exhausted, and she reluctantly agreed. After breakfast, Lawrence called Anna to prepare her for Gracie's visit before he headed to the farm.

Anna was relieved to hear that Olinda had finally relented and was allowing Gracie to stay with her and Edward, even if just for a short while. Olinda helped Lawrence pack clothes and a few of Gracie's favorite toys to take along. Then Olinda put James to bed, and before Lawrence and Gracie were even out the door, Olinda had crawled back under me and was asleep in no time. Maybe now, things would improve, I thought.

When Lawrence arrived home in the evenings, Olinda would tell him how terribly she missed their little girl, and she made him tell her every single thing Gracie had said or done that day. Lawrence assured her that Gracie was having the time of her life at the farm, helping Anna feed the chickens and cows. While he was busy fixing fences or loading hay bales, he would see Gracie running in the chicken yard, squealing as she carried a small bucket of feed, or playing with the newborn kittens under the awning of the tool shed.

Lawrence had lunch with Gracie when Anna prepared the noon meal, and he told Olinda that she asked about her mommy every day. This only made Olinda miss her more, but Lawrence told her that Gracie was having a lot of fun and the fresh air was wearing her out, and that this all helped her sleep very well at night for Anna. Hopefully, he told Olinda, James would settle down soon, so that Gracie would be back home in no time at all.

After just a few days, Lawrence could see that Olinda seemed better rested, even if she still didn't get much sleep at night. She appeared in even better spirits after she spoke with Anna on the telephone one day. She had called just to see how Gracie was getting along, and Anna put the telephone to Gracie's ear so that she could talk with her mommy. Olinda was so happy to hear her little girl's voice! She listened intently to Gracie telling her about the newborn kittens at the farm.

Shortly after that, Doc Bolen came by and gave Olinda a different medication for James, and soon Olinda was able to report to Lawrence that it seemed to be helping. After nearly a week, James finally seemed much calmer and had a better sleeping routine. Olinda was able to get her much needed rest, and Gracie returned home.

Olinda wasted no time devoting a part of every day to just Gracie. She played with the child for longer periods of time than she had previously, and she let Gracie help with kneading bread and baking cookies. She let Gracie hand her the powder tin when she changed James' diapers or bathed him, and she showed her how to help fold his tiny shirts and socks. Gracie was flourishing with all the attention, and Olinda couldn't get enough of her—she had missed her so much. Since James was doing so much better and had established a better sleeping pattern, Olinda was back to her pleasant self, too.

One day I heard Felicity and Ollie come into the house, and then Gracie and her little cousin played with some blocks on the floor while the two women talked. Felicity told Olinda that after almost five years, they were expecting a baby again. She confided to Olinda that she had thought she would never carry another child, because they had been trying so hard for the past few years with no success. But finally she was, and she and Wallace were overjoyed. The new baby would probably arrive sometime in October. Olinda congratulated her and said it would be nice for James to have a playmate, just like Ollie and Gracie enjoyed their time together.

Felicity also shared some news that Olinda had not heard yet. Albert had apparently begun dating a young girl who had moved to town recently to live with her aunt and uncle. Her name was Caroline. Felicity said that they had only met her once—at church with Albert the previous Sunday.

Olinda was overjoyed to hear this news. She told Felicity how happy she was and how she had hoped and prayed that Albert would meet someone. Olinda went on to say that she wished Albert would drop by now that things had settled down with baby James, because he had not met his new nephew yet. Olinda suggested that she might invite them to dinner on Sunday.

Felicity said that was a wonderful idea, but she offered to have the couples at her house, since Olinda had the new baby, and include Anna and Edward, too. Felicity said she had been feeling well in her pregnancy and that someday she might ask Olinda to return the favor, after her own second child was born. Olinda agreed and offered to bring food to add to the meal, since, after all, it had been her idea.

Then Olinda mentioned that she needed to call Father Duquette to set up a date for James' baptism. Gracie's had been performed just a week after her birth, but with James' feeding and sleeping issues, Olinda had put it off. Now that things were back to normal, she wanted to talk to the priest and settle on a date so she could let them all know when they could witness his baptism.

Felicity suggested killing two birds with one stone

and having the baptism the same day as the luncheon. Olinda said that would be wonderful, as long as Felicity didn't mind hosting it, and Felicity assured her that it would be her pleasure. Olinda promised to let her know once she had checked with the priest about his schedule.

Shortly after Felicity and Ollie left, Olinda called the priest, who agreed to perform the baptism on Sunday after late mass. That taken care of, she fed lunch to the children and put them down for naps. Gracie whined and said no, but Olinda insisted, because the little girl had woken up at the crack of dawn when Lawrence left the house. She said Gracie would never make it to suppertime if she didn't at least lie down awhile to rest. Despite her protests, Gracie must have fallen asleep, because the house was soon quiet.

I felt Olinda lie down on me, and then I heard the murmuring of her afternoon devotions and the clicking of her rosary beads, which had become her routine since James' birth. A short time later, the beads were silent and her soft snores enveloped the room as she, too, got a good hour of much needed rest.

A loud knock at the door startled Olinda, and she jerked awake, shaking the bed as she did so. She hurried out of the room to answer the door before the caller could knock again and perhaps wake the children.

I heard Olinda speaking to someone, a voice

I did not recognize. The woman was congratulating Olinda on the birth of her new child. As I listened, Olinda asked how this person knew she had recently had a baby. The visitor was very vague, not really offering a direct answer to the question.

As Olinda made excuses to the unknown woman, she must have tried to shut the door, but the woman persisted and requested a favor from Olinda. She said that she had recently lost a child and that she was very sorrowful because of it. She asked Olinda to please pray for her and to take this lovely white handkerchief. Olinda was instructed to burn it after three days, and then bury the ashes. The woman said only then could she be at peace and go to heaven.

Olinda was at a loss for words. She most likely thought this was a strange request, but she apparently took the handkerchief as a way to get the woman to leave her home. She promised to do as the woman wished. The stranger finally took her leave after assurances from Olinda that she would do as she had promised.

Olinda must have been watching her retreat through the yard when, all of a sudden, I heard her let out a strangled cry, followed by the sound of her footsteps as she ran to the door. She clicked the bolt loudly and then scurried around, and I could hear her drawing all the curtains in the front rooms tightly closed.

Immediately, Olinda got on the telephone, telling the operator to ring up Anna. Once she was connected and after making sure no one was listening to their conversation, she related her story in great detail, adding what she saw when the woman left her house. Olinda was overwrought, because it had indeed been a very strange incident, and her words made very little sense to me. As best I could, I tried to make out just what Olinda was telling her mother through her tears.

From what I could understand, Olinda thought that the woman was a gypsy selling her wares or a beggar looking for food, and she had tried to shoo the woman away. After the woman had given her well-wishes regarding the birth of James and had made her strange request, Olinda said she couldn't get rid of the woman fast enough, because she would not explain how she knew that Olinda had just had a baby. Olinda said it felt ominous that a stranger would just come to her home and congratulate her. She said it made her feel unsafe and on guard.

After Olinda agreed to the woman's strange request and observed her departure, what Olinda saw next sounded altogether otherworldly and grotesque. And that was what had caused her such alarm.

As Olinda watched the woman leave her yard, she saw her sit down on the stump of an old oak tree out near the front gate—one that Heiney had cut down years ago. The trunk was so large that two people could sit on it comfortably. The woman apparently had sat on the stump, placed her hands over her ears, lifted her head right off her shoulders, and sat it down on the stump next to her. Olinda said that the image was still burned into her brain and that every time she closed her eyes she still saw the strange vision. She told Anna she thought she must have been hallucinating.

Up until that moment, Olinda had not noticed anything in the woman's manner to indicate that she was not actually a person. She said the woman was dressed a little bit old-fashioned, but it had not occurred to Olinda that she might not have been physically real—was perhaps an apparition of some sort. A short time later, Olinda had looked out and had seen that the woman was gone—and Olinda wondered if she had dreamt the whole incident.

The handkerchief that remained in her hand, however, assured her that it had not been a dream. Olinda was beside herself, but after a while she grew quiet as she listened to Anna's reply, which seemed to calm her down.

Later, after she had hung up, I could hear her sniffling and mumbling for a short while, but then nothing more after that. I would learn no more about the story until later that evening.

I3

That night, while the family slept, I thought back on what had happened earlier that day. After the strange woman left the house and Olinda had talked with Anna, Olinda seemed very unsettled. She puttered around the house, not seeming to finish any one task. She shushed the children after they awoke from their naps if they fussed at all. It was as if she had something on her mind and didn't want her thoughts interrupted.

When Lawrence got home, he asked about supper, and Olinda told him that Anna and Edward would be arriving soon with their meal. He questioned why they were bringing supper, and Olinda simply said that her mother had offered to bring some chicken soup she had made and that they would eat when her parents arrived. Lawrence commented that when he left the farm, he noticed that Anna was busy in the kitchen, and that she hadn't come to the door to tell him goodbye like she normally did, but he hadn't given it much thought. I could vaguely hear Olinda telling Lawrence about the stranger's visit, but they were much too far away—near the back of the house—for me to hear clearly all that was said.

When Edward and Anna arrived, they all sat down to the meal and made small talk before any mention was made of the events of the day. After the children had been put to bed, and once the two couples had settled comfortably in the parlor, it was Anna who brought up the subject of Olinda's visitor.

It turned out that Anna herself had been visited by such a woman years earlier, shortly after she had given birth to Albert. Olinda gasped! She said she had wondered why Anna was so insistent about not discussing the subject at length over the telephone, but had wanted to come into town so they could continue the discussion over supper. Anna replied that it was something she wanted to explain in person, and that she felt relieved to talk about it and finally get it off her chest. At the time it happened, only Edward and Mary had known about it.

Anna told Lawrence and Olinda that she had felt unsettled, much like Olinda, but that she had completed the task as the woman had asked and then never heard anything more from her again. She wondered why the visitor had come again, visiting Olinda after the birth of her own second child, also a son. She declared that she had followed the visitor's wishes, so the woman should have been able to rest in peace.

Anna asked Olinda to relate the entire story to her once more. After Olinda had finished her account, Anna agreed that the details of what had happened were almost exactly the same, that even Olinda's description of the woman's appearance matched that of her own visitor exactly. The two couples tried to come up with a reasonable explanation, but none could be found.

Anna mentioned that at the time of her own experience with the strange visitor, she remembered hearing a story about a woman who had lived in Parrie many years ago. It told of a woman who had gone mad after the death of her infant son. For some reason, she blamed herself for his death, and although she had another child at home to care for, she had committed suicide by jumping off the bluff above the town. As she tumbled the nearly 100 feet from the top of the bluff, she fell across some tightly stretched barbed wire near the ravine below and was beheaded. It was a terrible tragedy—and the talk of the town.

This particular incident had apparently happened in the mid 1800s, long before Anna was even born. Mary, in whom Anna had confided at the time, had difficulty remembering the details, because she would have been a very young child herself at the time of the tragedy.

Anna's story had remained buried for all these years until the phone call this afternoon from Olinda, which brought the chilling tale back once more. There was no verification that these two strange women were one and the same, but the unique circumstances surrounding the visits and the similar descriptions of the visitors had everyone agreeing it was probable.

At the end of the evening, it was decided that there would be no harm in Olinda carrying out the woman's wishes, just as Anna had done years ago. Hopefully, this would put an end to it, and nothing more would be heard from her again. Anna mentioned that she herself had always had a way with things, that she had experienced premonitions of certain events in her lifetime. She felt that that was the reason the woman had come to her in the first place, because the woman sensed that Anna's mind was open to things of that nature.

Olinda assured her that she had never experienced anything of the sort before and hoped she never would again. Since the haunting experience seemed to reveal a pattern, Olinda said she hoped that since both she and Anna had met with the woman, maybe this poor soul would finally be at peace. Olinda hoped she would not present herself to a third family member—thinking of Gracie—at some time in the future.

Anna told Olinda not to worry, because she had a feeling deep in her heart that following through with the request would put an end to it. She said that at the time of her own encounter, she had felt that something wasn't quite right—perhaps she had missed something when fulfilling the request. Maybe this time Olinda would get it right, and the woman would finally leave them be.

Anna said that she had felt a sense of calm ever since she walked into the house this evening, almost as if someone or something was watching over them all. Olinda said she hoped she was right, that maybe Evangeline had found a way to come back and shelter them from harm. Anna laughed, saying that although Evangeline had talked of her life before and after moving to Parrie, she doubted that Evangeline had any unfinished business on this earth that would cause her to return in the afterlife.

Anna confirmed that she would come help on the day Olinda performed the task of burning the handkerchief and burying the ashes, just to make sure all went as planned. Hopefully they would truly close the book on this chapter, so to speak. Since this seemed to be the best way to handle the situation, no more was spoken on the subject that night.

The next day, I overheard Olinda talking to Felicity as they made plans for Sunday's lunch after late mass and the baptism. Once again, Olinda thanked her for hosting the party at her home. She agreed to make a few dishes for the luncheon, including two pies for dessert, since pie was a favorite of Albert's. Olinda was excited about getting to know this new young lady, because Albert very rarely brought anyone to meet the family.

After Felicity left, Olinda realized that the burning of the handkerchief and burying of its ashes was to be on Sunday, too, because that would be the third day after the woman's visit. She called Anna to talk with her about it, because with the baptism after mass and the plans for Sunday's lunch, Olinda was worried about whether the event with the handkerchief could even take place. She was concerned about having to leave the party at some point to come back to the house to carry out the task.

Anna apparently thought that it would be simple enough to do: After lunch, the men would most likely play cards and the women would visit amongst themselves, so Anna and Olinda could leave for a few minutes with the excuse of going across the yard to change the baby out of his christening gown. Anna felt that would satisfy the others' curiosity, and the women agreed to mention their plans to Edward and Lawrence, so they could downplay the disappearance if anyone asked about it.

The events of that fateful Sunday would affect me in a way I could never have imagined, for what occurred on that day was truly my dream come true. How and why it happened may never be known, but I can tell you this—it changed me in a way I had thought absolutely impossible.

PART TWO

14

The day of my "awakening," as I came to call it, began like most days in the home of Olinda, Lawrence, and the children. They arose from sleep, Olinda a little earlier than Lawrence. Then before the children woke up, they went about getting ready for the day. On this particular day, they prepared food for the special lunch that was planned before they got the children ready for the baptism and late Sunday mass. After a quick breakfast, Lawrence entertained the children while Olinda finished her preparations, and I heard them talking as Olinda packed the pies and other dishes in a basket for Lawrence to take over to Wallace and Felicity's house before they left for church.

I began to reminisce about all that had happened to me. I have shared so many experiences with this family since my early days with Anna and Edward. I had heard so many sounds around me: voices, animals, thunder and rain, birds, insects, train whistles, music and honking car horns, among others. I couldn't begin to name all of them, and I only learned what these sounds were called when the family referred to them.

I had felt cold, warm, wet, and dry. I had felt the gentle breezes and whipping winds, the touch of hands lifting me or pulling me. There were so many sensations I had experienced and come to understand, even though they were not always named by someone's voice. I was almost like a child, learning over the years while growing to adulthood, much like Olinda and her brothers, who were mere children when I joined the family.

What happened to me on that day—April 27, 1930—was more wonderful than I could have imagined. I only knew what day it was because of something I had overheard in passing. Now I will try my best to relate the events as they took place.

I heard the family leave the house to go to mass. Much later, Anna and Olinda came into the house, and I could hear them planning how and where to carry out the spirit woman's wishes. I heard Olinda walk into the bedroom to change James out of his christening gown, then she laid him on top of me on the bed.

After Olinda had finished changing James, she told Anna that she had the handkerchief, and she suggested that maybe they should head out the back door and burn and bury the ashes well away from the house. She remarked that she wanted to bury them someplace where they wouldn't be disturbed, possibly underneath the old weeping willow tree in the back yard. The drooping branches of the tree itself would also hide their actions from curious neighbors, and they would not be able to be seen from Wallace and Felicity's house if anyone happened to peek outside.

Olinda told Anna that she had some kerosene and matches ready, as well as a small shovel to dig a hole in which to bury the ashes. She had decided to use an old coal bucket for burning the handkerchief, to contain it, and then they could dump the ashes into the hole they had dug.

Anna said she felt that is where she had gone wrong years ago: She had burned and buried the ashes near the edge of her garden, and the ashes had inadvertently been disturbed when the garden was plowed up the following spring. Anna agreed that burying them near the trunk of the tree was the best solution to prevent this, because no one would be digging up the earth under the weeping willow.

As far as I know, that is what they did.

Anna said that she hoped this 27th day of April, 1930, would be the last anyone would hear of the ghostly woman and burning handkerchiefs. During these two women's lifetimes, no more was mentioned about the incident ever again, or at least not that I heard.

Anna and Olinda went back outside to perform the task. Olinda left baby James, who was falling asleep, in his crib. I thought I heard someone speaking to the child, but I could not be sure. I strained to hear, trying to determine if it was Anna or Olinda, but the voice sounded much softer and quieter than I had ever heard from either of them. It was so faint it was almost like the wind whispering softly, and it gave me a chill.

My fears were confirmed when Olinda and Anna came back into the house to retrieve James. I realized that it couldn't have been either of them speaking. But whose voice was it? As far as I knew, no one else had been in the house. I would never know the answer.

Olinda gathered up James in his blanket, and she and Anna left the house to go back next door.

A few moments after they left, I began to have the oddest sensations I had ever experienced. It was as if everything I had learned or known over the years had somehow intensified, had deeper meaning, or was of greater significance.

I had heard someone say that if walls could talk, what a tale they could tell. But since walls and other objects have no voice, no one knows what goes on behind closed doors. I guess that is how I felt sometimes: Much like a fly on the wall, I heard things, but I could not tell the things I overheard or even begin to understand everything going on around me. The secrets and stories told within these walls were all safe with me, for I could not repeat them.

I still did not understand why I was able to experience so many things and why the sensations were so much stronger on this day. Did it have something to do with the strange woman's visit a few days ago and the burning and burying of the handkerchief today? Was it possible that the woman had returned? Had it been her voice that I heard?

I will never know for sure, but as I pondered these things, a sensation that was definitely different and stronger came over me. It was almost as if an electric current had taken hold, and all my fibers quivered. I experienced a heightened sense of awareness. The clock ticking at the bedside was much louder than I had ever noticed. Gracie's cat, which often jumped on top of me, was purring, and it seemed to be echoing deep within my being.

I literally felt as if my insides were swelling up, as if they were going to burst out, scattering into a million pieces. Then—all at once—I felt the deepest, hottest, brightest flash of what I realized could only be what the others all called light. It opened me up to a whole new level of perception.

I ... could ... see!

I had such a jumble of thoughts that it was nearly overwhelming. I heard Anna say one time that she fainted once and felt her life flash before her eyes. I wondered if this was what she meant.

Could I be dying? Not physically, but maybe in whatever realm I have existed since I came into being so many years ago? Would I cease to experience this day-to-day life I had come to know? I didn't really feel that way though—it was almost the exact opposite. It was more like I was being born—like a door had opened and let me come through.

I wondered if I was really going to be able to see everything that was before me now, or was this just a fleeting moment? I began to consider the possibilities this new awareness presented to me. I let my thoughts settle, and I absorbed it all as best I could.

To this day I cannot tell you how I knew I was actually seeing my surroundings. It was something I had so longed for, and yet I still couldn't believe it was happening. I glanced around the room, my vision landing in random places, not lingering very long on any one item, just taking it all in.

How could this be? Was it truly real, or was I having a dream like one of Gracie's? She often told Lawrence and Olinda in great detail about a castle with princesses, or about a nightmare she had had about a bogeyman under her bed.

All I know is that I was experiencing things I had only imagined. Yet I couldn't quite grasp it all. I guessed that it was perhaps like something else

I had overheard one day, a conversation between Anna and the Mrs. many years ago. They talked about someone who had just awoken from a coma. One day, the person just woke up after being unconscious for a very long time—like an awakening from a very deep slumber.

I glanced at the doorway that led to the hallway, past the front door, and beyond to the parlor where my vision grew dim. It seemed that my newfound sight was confined mainly to this one room, which made sense, since this was the room my form was in.

In addition to the bed, there were other items I had heard Olinda and Lawrence talk about using every day, and now I was seeing them for the very first time. There was the chifforobe with the mirror on one side, where I had heard them talk as they dressed each day. I knew this had a mirror, because there was a reflection, and I had heard Olinda explaining to Gracie what a reflection was.

In this reflection, I came to know what I looked like. I had heard people say over the years that I was beautiful. When Anna had stitched my fabric together, she said she followed a pattern called Grandmother's Fan. Now I could see exactly what that meant.

The pieces of color, scraps sewn and arranged in such a way that they came to a point and fanned out, were laid out over the whole of me in a pattern of squares or blocks. In between, there were strips of no color—white is the word that came to me. Some of the cloth was plain, and some had designs that seemed to dance in the warm sunlight coming through the window. Some pieces were bold or flashy, and others were muted or pale. It all made an arrangement across me.

I saw the stitches that Anna and the Mrs. and Olinda had made, tiny and fine, and the plump little designs that were left between and around the stitches. Oh my! I felt so proud! It was marvelous to witness my own appearance for the first time.

My gaze moved on around the room. There were some items I was unsure of, and I would have to wait to see them being used to understand what they were. But as I was looking around at the furniture and at the many decorations on the walls—all the things that I had shared space with these past few years, it occurred to me that there was truly only one thing I wished to see. I could not wait to gaze into the faces of my family. I longed for them to return home for this reason! I couldn't even imagine what they would look like.

For the rest of that day, I thought hard about everything in my line of sight, seeing objects and trying to make up names for what I thought they were.

Gracie's cat, called Pelagie, was named after one of Lawrence's grandmothers, who apparently had had hair the same salt and pepper color as the cat. Pelagie was curled up on top of me, so that was an easy one to figure out, because she purred just as she always had. She wasn't very big, and I had the feeling my family would be bigger, since I barely felt her lying on top of me. When Olinda and Lawrence stretched out underneath me at night, their bodies took up quite a bit more space than Pelagie did.

I glanced at the clock ticking at the bedside and, since I had my vision now, I saw that the little sticks of metal—hands, I think they were called—had moved. That is when I realized how my family marked the passage of time. Olinda would wind this clock every night and set the alarm to wake them in the morning.

I saw the calendar hanging on the wall. Although I couldn't read the letters and numbers there, I had a sense that that was what it was, because I had often heard Olinda refer to it. The calendar hung above her sewing machine, and she marked it to show when she needed to have her projects completed.

The sewing machine was easy to figure out. It was covered with material like me that she was in the middle of crafting into something new. I had heard the sound it makes coming from the exact corner where it was located.

As I spent the day studying my surroundings, I wondered why I had gained the sense of sight—and why now? I really felt that it must have something to do with the strange visitor and the handkerchief burning, but I told myself not to dwell on it any longer. Being able to see seemed surreal, but I was going to enjoy it for however long it lasted, whether for one day or forever.

As the day was coming to a close, I noticed my vision dimming. Because I had no sense of day or night, I really and truly thought that my sense of sight was to be very short-lived. But when the family came home and lights came on in the house, I realized that day had turned to night, but that I could still see.

The moment I had been waiting for had finally arrived. After hearing the sounds of Lawrence and Olinda settling the children down for the night, I saw them come into the bedroom. I gazed upon their faces for the first time, and I was totally unprepared. They looked nothing like Pelagie the cat.

They were more wonderful than I could ever have imagined. They moved about the room quickly as if they were fluid, their bodies seeming to float around the room as they prepared for sleep. The two of them talked to one another about the baptism and lunch that day, but I took no time to listen as I gazed at their faces and bodies.

My thoughts were all jumbled as I looked first from Olinda's face and then to Lawrence's. So this is what my people looked like! If I were to guess, I'd say they were a handsome couple. Lawrence was a little bit larger than Olinda, and neither one had hair anything like Pelagie's. Their hair only covered the tops of their heads, although Olinda had a little bit more on her head than Lawrence did.

I watched as they got ready for bed, and Olinda pulled something else on to wear; I had often heard her call it a nightgown. They turned out the light, and both knelt beside the bed as they always did, saying their prayers at the end of a long day. And as they crawled between me and the sheets underneath, I experienced a totally different feeling than I had on previous nights. On this night, I felt that I was a comfort to them, a protector of the night. Before long, they were both asleep.

I had so much to think about that night! And I could not wait until morning, excited about the possibility that the children might pay a visit to the room.

15

I spent much of the next few days observing every movement and facial expression of Lawrence and Olinda whenever they were in the bedroom. At night, when the lights were out and the house was dark, I watched the shadows on the walls, created by the moonlight as it came in through the windows.

I joyfully greeted each new morning as another gift. I was still so delighted that I had acquired the ability to see, and I wanted to enjoy it for however long it lasted.

I began to watch and wait for anyone else to come into the bedroom. Although I could not see other rooms besides this one, I could look down the hall past the front door and into the parlor. The house was small enough that I could hear most conversations held in these two rooms, as well as bits and pieces from the dining room and kitchen nearby. The children's rooms were near the back of the house, I supposed, and I had never been able to hear any of the family's exchanges from there.

By this time, I had memorized every facet of Olinda and Lawrence's appearance. I saw her change out of her nightgown in the morning, put on a dress and shoes, and, depending on the weather, stockings and a sweater—to keep her warm, I assumed.

I loved to watch Olinda as she used the hairbrush on the dresser to brush her hair. Sometimes at night, she fashioned it into sections all wound together, pinning it up on her head with little bent wires that she first put in her mouth. It fascinated me to watch this process, and I wondered if the children had hair like this, too. In the mornings, she would take out the little pins, and her hair would be slightly curled and fluffy as she brushed it.

When she dressed for the day, most of the time she put on an additional article of clothing—an apron with pockets into which she put her rosary and a fresh handkerchief. I noticed that on Sundays before mass, she didn't put the apron on, but that she would put it on when she came back home. I wondered if this apron was something she only wore when she was cooking or cleaning, possibly to keep her other clothes from getting soiled.

I watched Lawrence as he got ready for the day, putting on his pants and shirt and heavy work boots. I had always identified these boots with the sound they made on the floor, even before I could see. I always knew when he came into the house, because of his heavy footsteps in those boots.

His hat that hung on a hook near the door was always the last thing he grabbed before he left the house. He took less time on his appearance than Olinda did, barely running a comb through his short hair, and if I didn't look quickly, he would be dressed and gone before I knew it.

I never saw him put a rosary in any of his pockets, but he did put several other things in them. One item looked like a miniature version of the bedside ticking clock, except this one was on a chain of sorts that he hooked to something on his clothes so that it was attached to him. I later realized that this was the pocket watch that Olinda had given him that first Christmas, when they had gotten engaged. He always carried something else with him, too. It was a little larger than the miniature clock, but it still fit in his hand. I think it might have held his money, because he often checked it and asked Olinda if she needed any cash for the day before he put it in his pants pocket. I came to understand that this money was what they used to buy things for themselves.

Then there was something that he always had with him that I only saw him use once; he called it a pocketknife. He opened it up to reveal a sharp, shiny edge that glinted in the sunlight spilling through the window. Then he ran it across the frayed ends of his shoelaces before knotting them together. He said that way they would hold until he could buy new ones. I thought the pocketknife must come in handy for him throughout the day.

As it turned out, my first glimpse of Gracie and James took several more days. The children were not usually allowed in their parents' bedroom, but Gracie occasionally followed her mother into the room when Olinda came in to get something. Olinda, devout as she was, always wanted to have her rosary with her, but on some mornings she forgot to put it in her apron pocket, and she would come back to the bedroom to get it.

That is what happened on the day I finally got to see the children. By then I had every freckle and mole of Olinda and Lawrence memorized, so it was not a huge surprise to me that when I did see the youngsters for the first time, they were like miniature versions of their parents—only the faces were reversed. To my surprise, Gracie was almost the mirror image of her father, and James, well, he looked very much like Olinda. Gracie was a bit taller than James, also slimmer, and her hair was hanging down with a pretty ribbon holding it back from her face. As Olinda carried James, I realized that he was a plump baby, with hair that was short like his father's.

I had no comparison yet as to what other people looked like, and I began to wonder if this was how things were for other families. I came to realize that I didn't much care. As long as I knew my people, that was all that mattered to me.

One day, I got the best surprise: After all my years of wondering about her, I got to see Anna! She and Edward dropped by the house when they made a trip to town to have their corn ground into feed at the mill. Edward stayed a short while and then left to run other errands, but Anna stayed and had a nice long visit with Olinda. I really didn't expect Anna to come into the bedroom, but Olinda asked her to come and see the progress she was making on her latest sewing project—one that had kept her busy most days when the children were napping. It was a wedding dress she had been asked to make for Lawrence's youngest sister, who was to be married next month.

As they walked down the hall, Olinda told Anna that hopefully, if things moved along for Albert and Caroline, she might just be asked to make another one next year. Anna told her not to count her chickens yet, but that it would be a nice turn of events if it did happen. It seemed that everyone in the family was very fond of Caroline.

When the two women came into the room, I had to look twice. Oh my! Anna looked like a slightly different version of Olinda! It appeared that everyone looked like someone in their family. Or at least in this family anyway. And yes, it was wonderful to finally see what my maker looked like! I had dreamt of this moment for so long, and yet when it happened, it was as if I had always known that was what she would look like. I imagined her hands upon me once more, as when they had run across my form as she stitched me together.

I reveled in those moments while she was in the room with Olinda, looking at the dress. My attention was directed only toward Anna, for I doubted that such an occasion would come again anytime soon. Because I knew they might not stay long, as they laid the dress on top of me so that Olinda could show Anna the details, I studied her profile. I memorized everything about her, so that in quiet times I could think about her—holding the memory of what she looked like deep within my being.

She had pale eyes of the loveliest color, not at all like Olinda's darker ones, but an unusual shade that set off her face well. When she ran her hands down the dress, she touched my soul, and I shivered as I remembered her tender touch when she had formed me. When they had finished looking at the dress, Olinda laid it aside, and they left the room.

Neither Olinda nor Anna had any inkling that I was able to hear and see them. I was so overcome with emotion, being able to see them together in the same room. I was as content as I could be, and I felt almost like I was in a trance.

It was then I had a strange, deep feeling, and I came to the realization that maybe this was the feeling that people called love. I felt like I might burst from it, and I didn't quite know what to make of this. It took me most of the day to feel calmer again.

That night, as the family settled down to sleep and the house was quiet, I realized I had nothing left to wish for, at least not for myself. I had so longed to see my surroundings, and that had happened, just like I had dreamed. I had wished to see the faces of my family, and I had been able to do that, too.

Now I wondered if my purpose might be to hope and dream that my family would live long, healthy, and happy lives. Hopefully, one day when the children—Gracie and James and any others who might join this family—would grow older like Anna, I would still be here to give them comfort and warmth. I could only wish that would be the case.

16

The years rolled by quickly and, as the saying goes, time stands still for no one, including me. I had come to realize just how much this family meant to me. There were so many times over the years that I wished for ways I could show them, but that was not meant to be, for I could not initiate anything.

Although I could not express it, I had become aware of how fond I was of each and every member of this family. The good times and the bad times they experienced were a part of my existence, just as they were of theirs, even though they had no idea that I was involved right along with them. I longed for a way to let them know just how much I had come to love them, but that was not possible.

The Great Depression had long since passed, but its aftereffects lasted well into the next decade, when war restricted the family's livelihood once again. Over the years, the entire family had undergone many, many changes.

Albert and Caroline had been married for more than ten years now. They had a set of twin boys, Melvin and Alvin, age 9, who were followed by a daughter, Rita, two years later. The family had moved into a house across the street from Olinda and Lawrence.

Albert's cabinetmaking business had flourished, but at the onset of the second war, his business took a hard hit, and he had to make significant changes to stay afloat. His two apprentices were both gone: One had no choice, because he was drafted; the other ran off to join a traveling circus to avoid the draft. Albert stayed busy though, selling scrap lumber and cutting firewood that could be sold or traded to homes and businesses for ration coupons, for coal had become scarce. He also had orders from the government for logs for the CCC camp down south, and a few from factories in St. Louis where he trucked his loads on a weekly basis. The timberland at the family farm above the bluff proved profitable enough to keep him afloat.

Wallace and Felicity's son Ollie was a young man now, 20 years old this year. He followed in his father's footsteps and had begun working at the quarry after high school graduation. His younger brother, Harry, age 15, idolized Ollie and loved to tag along after him. Ollie had escaped being drafted in World War II because of a bad knee, injured when playing high school basketball. He still walked with a slight limp, although it didn't slow him down much.

Wallace put in many long hours at the quarry, because much of his workforce had been drafted or had enlisted. He made adjustments as best he could to keep the doors open. Felicity had begun working there, too, keeping books and even driving trucks now and then, as the need arose. With Ollie working there full-time and Harry helping after school, the quarry kept their family quite busy.

Anna and Edward were enjoying their twilight years, so to speak. Edward had developed a heart condition and was now right at 70 years of age. He had retired from farming, and although they still lived at the farm, he did not participate in its day-to-day operation as much as he would have liked. The fields were rented to neighboring farmers for planting wheat, beans, or corn. The rent money he received was used for upkeep of his outbuildings and other basic expenses.

Edward and Anna had invested some of the money they inherited from Evangeline, and while they had lost some of it during the Depression, he had wisely put much of it in savings rather than stocks, so they were not affected too deeply. Luckily, the town bank had stayed solvent, although some banks had folded during the Depression.

Edward had also kept a few animals in the barns just so he still felt like a farmer, and he had hung onto his tractor so he could till up the garden for Anna when it was time to plant her vegetables and flowers. But most of his time these days was spent tinkering with the first car he had ever purchased, with plans to get it running and restored to its former glory.

Anna still enjoyed her quilting, gardening, and canning—everything she cared for most in life besides her family. The pair lived frugally, even though by most standards they were fairly well-off. She loved living in the wide open spaces of the farm where she had grown up and lived as a child, and she still loved to cook.

She and Edward would often host big Sunday dinners, when the whole family would gather around the oversized farmhouse table to enjoy a meal together. Meals consisted of the animals they raised and slaughtered and the fruits and vegetables they grew. Edward had more time to hunt now, as long as he didn't overexert himself, and he often came home with deer, rabbits, or squirrels that she would prepare for them to eat. Both Edward and Anna enjoyed fishing for catfish and crappie in the pond behind the barn. The couple now lived an easy, somewhat slower lifestyle.

But my family, the ones I had grown to love with all my being, had undergone the most changes of all. Lawrence suffered a series of setbacks that left him unable to work. He had gone back to working on his boat shortly after the lean years of the Great Depression. Then one morning, he awoke with chills and an off-and-on fever that never truly went away. He had always felt fatigued and somewhat cold, and for years he attributed that to his job on the river. But as his illness progressed, he would dress in layers and layers of clothes, in spite of the warmer weather. Finally, one day Olinda insisted that he see the doctor, who ordered him into the hospital in Robertsville for tests.

When they got the test results back, Lawrence was diagnosed with a chronic blood disorder that left him severely anemic. Although this was a serious illness, because his condition was chronic rather than acute, he was told that he could live a long time if he made regular visits to the doctor and took his medicine as ordered. He would also need periodic blood transfusions if his blood levels got too low. With Lawrence in such a weakened state, Olinda had her hands full taking care of him, along with monthly visits to his doctor in Robertsville, running the household, keeping up with her sewing business, and worrying about their two teenagers, Gracie and James. While Lawrence didn't seem to be getting worse and eventually went into remission from his disease, he still spent a lot of his days in bed, lying right under me.

My ability to see had not diminished over the past 15 years, and I was able to notice great changes in Lawrence's appearance. He was no longer the strapping young man he had once been, but a smaller, slighter version of his former self. As time passed, he spent less time in bed, but he was still not able to captain his tugboat. The family was eventually forced to sell it, much to his dismay.

The children, Gracie and James, had undergone transformations themselves. Over the years, they had gone from a toddler and a baby to young adults in what seemed to me like the blink of an eye. Although I did not see them often, because they rarely came into their parents' bedroom, I would get fleeting glimpses of them as they passed through the hallway to the front door or sat in the one corner of the parlor that I could see. Gracie had grown into quite a beautiful young lady, and James a handsome, strong-looking young man.

Lawrence's father had passed away peacefully in his sleep one night around Christmas in 1943. Lawrence's youngest brother, Michael, found him when he returned from a run with his boat. Shortly after the funeral, the family met at Emile's house to clear it out and choose what they wanted to keep. His father had lived frugally, and there were not many belongings to go through. Lawrence was very pleased to get an old lantern that had been his grandfather's, along with one of his father's pocket watches. He thought they were things he could pass down to Gracie and James someday.

The war was a hardship on the family as well. World War II had brought many sacrifices, especially with Lawrence unable to work. Olinda divided her time between two jobs: She had taken a job at the new shoe factory in Elmira, just a few miles away, where she worked making Army boots to be used for servicemen; and she sewed late into the night on projects for people in Parrie. Still, Olinda's work and their ration coupons weren't quite enough for the family. Anna and Edward supported them through what was another very distressing time in their lives. Olinda and Lawrence often mentioned that they didn't think they could have survived were it not for Anna and Edward's help.

Olinda commented one day about all the bad luck their family was having, and she said she often wondered if she should have carried out the task of burning the handkerchief for the spirit woman. Maybe it had brought a curse on them, she told Lawrence one day. Lawrence said he thought it unlikely, but Olinda still had her doubts. She wondered if maybe she had not done something right, as Anna had mentioned about her own failed attempt years ago.

Gracie, ever the sweetheart of the family, graduated from high school just before the end of the war, and she was determined to go to school to become a nurse. After seeing her father suffer so much and caring for him as much as she could while Olinda worked, she realized that this was something she would find fulfilling. She was such a compassionate and loving young lady. I often wished I could see her as she worked as a nurse's aide at the hospital, a job she had taken on while still in school.

On days when Lawrence stayed in bed, I was witness to her loving care of him. She brought him trays of food, and she helped him down the hallway into a chair in the parlor. I imagined she would make a very competent nurse. James sometimes helped his father, too. I witnessed his strength firsthand one day: Lawrence was feeling very weak, and James had to lift and carry him to the car because Lawrence didn't have the strength to walk, even with support. I often thought that the family's care of their father did more good for him than any of the medicine that he took.

James had begun working for the town newspaper at a young age, starting out with delivering papers to the townspeople. Later, he was given more responsibility. He helped with folding, printing, or whatever needed to be done at the office. Early on, he willingly handed over his weekly paycheck, meager as it was, to Olinda to help with the expenses at home.

Olinda felt guilty about taking her son's money, but she realized that they needed most of it just to get by. She also hated that her parents had to support them so much. She knew that Anna and Edward did it willingly and that they would do it for any of their children, but it still upset her that her family needed so much help.

Unbeknownst to James though, Olinda set up a savings account at the bank in his name, and she put a small portion of each check into the account. That way, his hard work was not all for them. The small amounts would add up, and someday he would have money for beginning his own life journey.

In the fall of 1945, as the country was about to begin its recovery after the war, Gracie was ready to begin her studies to become a nurse. She planned to attend the college in Clarkstown, just a little more than an hour away from home. Because of the distance, she would travel to Clarkstown on the bus that passed through Parrie, taking with her all the clothes and other things she would need for the school year.

Olinda had been trying to set aside money for Gracie's nursing studies, ever since Gracie had revealed that as her intention when she was still in high school, but Olinda was still short on the amount needed to pay Gracie's tuition. And Olinda dreaded asking her parents for help.

As it turned out, Gracie—smart as she was—was able to earn a scholarship that paid for a good portion of her schooling. Gracie had also found a very reasonable room at a boarding house just a few blocks from the college, and she and her friend Shirley, who was attending the same college to become a teacher, planned on rooming together and sharing the rent.

To help pay for her living expenses, Gracie had gotten a job at the hospital in Clarkstown, which was near the campus, and she would be able to work there as a nurse's aide. Things finally seemed to be falling into place.

After all this time, I was noticing changes in myself, too, and feeling the effects of years of use. Since I could see and not just feel, I realized over time that I was beginning to look tattered. Olinda, with so much work to do around the house and her two jobs, had little time for mending me. After that first memorable washing, I had had many more over the years, and each one seemed to take a little bit away from me. Lawrence had taken advantage of my warmth and comfort a lot during his sick years, so I was showing signs of wear.

Just as the years of hard work for Olinda had seemed to age her, I was beginning to look old and worn out, too. I wasn't nearly as fluffy, there were several small holes and bare spots, and I was starting to look somewhat sad.

Nevertheless, I kept Lawrence and Olinda warm at night, and I must have still been useful, for I wasn't being replaced just yet. Sometimes though, as I grew thinner and flatter, I would be covered with another blanket on cold nights.

The following spring—1946—brought Gracie back home from college. She began working at the hospital in Robertsville as a nurse's aide again. Her job at school had ended for now, and she planned on going back to school and her job at the Clarkstown hospital when school resumed in the fall.

Gracie's life was a whirlwind. She started out early in the morning and left for work, then hurried home in the evening for a quick supper, and headed out with friends afterward several nights a week. They would visit the movie theater or the dance hall in town or sometimes the soda fountain at the drug store in Robertsville. Often on those nights, she did not come home until late. I knew about this because she would tell Olinda and Lawrence about it the next morning before leaving for work.

James kept busy, too, because his job at the newspaper, which was full-time in the summer, kept him going from morning till night. He did not let much grass grow under his feet, as Olinda would often say. When he wasn't working, he would occasionally spend time with his buddies, fishing in the river. Other times, he kept Lawrence company, because he knew his father was lonely while the family went about their days.

Lawrence was often left to his own devices, and he spent a lot of time alone while the others were gone. Olinda and Lawrence had some long talks late into the night about the situation, and she suggested that he try to get out of the house more, now that he was feeling a little better, maybe going for walks to get his strength back.

Lawrence asked Olinda if she thought he should talk to Albert about helping him in the shop with some of his smaller jobs. It would give him something to do and be a way to earn some money, and it would make him feel needed again, too. Olinda thought that was a wonderful idea. Lawrence talked with Albert and found that Albert was eager to hire him to help with the cabinetwork, now that he was getting busier again. Lawrence's mood improved a great deal after that, and he went to the shop a few hours a day, as much as he was able.

With the war now over, Olinda lost her job at the factory, because they cut back on making soldiers' boots. That meant that the money Lawrence made working with Albert was a very welcome addition to the family's finances.

On a warm Friday afternoon in the summer of that year, Gracie announced to Olinda and Lawrence that she and her friends were going to go watch the fireworks out by the ruins of the old fort near the river, since it was the Fourth of July weekend. This was something I had known about, but never witnessed in person. I had only heard the booming of the fireworks that were shot off in the distance. There were plans for a large gathering in the park area around the fort. Gracie said that she wanted to take a blanket to sit on, and Olinda told her to take me off the bed, since I was needing a good wash again anyway, and she wouldn't mind if the quilt got dirty.

Now I was in for another outing away from home—something I had not done for many years! This sounded like a good idea to me! My time out of the house recently had been limited to occasional trips out to the clothesline, where my vision was obscured by the buildings and trees. Although this satisfied my desire to see other things, I wanted to experience more.

That evening, just before dark, Gracie threw me into the old car and headed out to pick up several friends. I sat on the seat, gazing out the window as buildings and trees sped by. I had no idea there were so many buildings in town; it was something I had only been able to guess at.

Gracie stopped twice, and two other young ladies got into the vehicle—her school roommate, Shirley, and another girl named Faye. I remembered these girls from their younger days, because they had come into the house and I had heard their voices, but since they didn't come into Olinda and Lawrence's bedroom where I was, I had never seen them. They looked very little alike, and not at all like Gracie. Gracie was petite and slim, but these two were both taller, with Faye being the plumper of the two. She was actually quite fluffy, like I used to be.

It was beginning to get darker and the town had few street lights, so it was getting harder for me to see anything by the time the girls headed out of town. The car moved along the road as the three girls chatted about young men they knew, their jobs, and makeup—all things that didn't interest me at all.

When we arrived at the old fort, there must have been a lot of cars there, because Gracie said they would have to walk a ways to get to the field for a good view of the fireworks. The girls got out of the car after Gracie parked near a grove of trees, and Gracie grabbed me before they headed off. I had never been outside at night after dark, so this was a new experience.

They made their way to the entrance of the park near the old stone fort, and Gracie spread me out on the grass near several other blankets. They didn't sit on me right away, but Gracie threw her purse and the car keys down on top of me, and then the girls wandered around among the groups of people, talking and laughing.

As I looked around from my spot on the ground, I could see more cars heading into the area, their lights passing over me as they drove by. A few people had brought lanterns or flashlights to light the pathway. That helped me, too, for it was quite a dark night with very few stars, and cloud cover blocked the moon's glow.

As I gazed about the area, I could make out the ruins of the old fort a short distance away. I had heard about this place, because Olinda and Lawrence had driven by here when they were courting long ago, on their drive down by the river to watch the tugboats and visit at his parents' home. It was hard to see in the dim light, but I could just make out the crumbling rocks of the ancient fort built centuries ago.

Soon it was time for the festivities to begin, and the girls came back to sit down on me and watch, bringing several other friends with them. I could barely see around them all—just enough to see the brilliant fireworks display. The bright colors and shapes in the sky were quite a sight to behold, and I was overjoyed that they had brought me on the trip with them.

The noise was something else! Booming and crackling unlike anything I had ever heard—much louder than what I had heard from inside the house in previous years. There was a smoky haze hanging in the air, and I noticed that one of the girls was holding her nose and saying what a stink there was. I could only imagine what that was like, because I can't smell. The light show, however, was spectacular!

As the fireworks wound down, the girls sat there giggling and talking. Eventually, they got up to visit their friends again, leaving me to ponder all I had seen that night.

I have no idea how long I lay there in the grass, along with a few other forgotten blankets and personal belongings, while everyone continued visiting and talking a short distance away. Someone had lit a campfire, and a lot of people were singing songs and passing around jugs and bottles, sitting on other blankets and folding chairs that had been placed on the grass. The group was beginning to grow louder, but their voices faded into the night air, so it wasn't overpowering.

I liked the feeling of lying in the dark with just the few stars to look at, and I was thankful Gracie had not pulled me near the fire, where a stray spark might have gotten the best of me. Once the smoke had cleared from the fireworks, I was able to see that the moon had emerged from the clouds and was now shining quite brightly. The crowd was much quieter now, because several had gone home, but Gracie and her two friends and about a dozen others still sat around the fire, chatting quietly and enjoying the glowing embers.

Over near the entrance to the fort, I began to see shapes. At first it was difficult to see, and I definitely couldn't hear any sound coming from what I was seeing. It was as if all the sound had been sucked out of the air.

There appeared to be a carriage of some sort being pulled by horses. I had seen horses in town years ago when I was hung to dry on the clothesline, so I knew what they were. This carriage was pulling a wagon, and on the bed of the wagon was a long box. Other carriages followed, with people inside them, and I could see the people moving and talking. But no sound was coming from the procession at all. I could see the horses' hooves moving up and down, and the wheels turning on the carriages, and a few lone horses with riders moving through the group—but not a sound was heard. This seemed most strange to me!

I heard a dog barking in the distance, and I could still hear the group around the fire. This procession was passing so close to everyone, and yet not one person near the fire seemed to acknowledge it. I wanted to shout to the others so that they would see it, too—but of course I could not speak. I did see a few partygoers looking in that direction, but if they saw it, they did not share the news; they just kept on with their conversations, laughing and talking without a care in the world.

It seemed so strange to me that I could hear the young people's conversations, but I could not hear a single sound from this procession as it made its way past the old fort entrance. I had no idea where it was headed, but the procession seemed to have a specific destination, because they all stayed in a single line of riders and carriages.

Just then, a new fellow drove into the area and

jumped out of his car. He exclaimed that he had just seen something quite strange. As he told the party-goers what he saw, I realized that it was exactly what I had seen.

Everyone laughed at the fellow and told him that he must have had too much to drink. He explained that he hadn't had a drop, because he had just gotten off work from his evening shift at the factory and driven out to the fort in hopes that he could still take part in the fun. But no one believed him. They still accused him of being drunk, because they hadn't seen any of what he proclaimed to see. How could they not, he asked, because it had to have passed right by them!

He insisted that he saw a group of carriages and horses, but that the whole formation had been as if it was a silent picture show. They all kept teasing him, so he finally sat down without another word and stared deeply into the fire, clearly troubled by what he had seen.

This made me think even harder as I wondered about this. At least one or two of the partygoers should have been able to see it, because I had seen it. The nearby dog had barked as if it might have, but not one other person there had experienced what I, this new fellow, and possibly the dog had seen that night. It was all very puzzling to me, and something I would think about for the rest of the night.

We finally left to head home, and Gracie and her friends chattered excitedly all the way back to town about the fun they had had, laughing and joking about the story the young man—Jeb, they called him—had told.

Gracie left me on the floor in the parlor when she came home that night, so as not to disturb her parents, because they were already asleep when she got back to the house. As I lay in the moonlight looking around the parlor and taking in all there was to see in that room, I relived my experience that night. It was something I could not forget or put aside. It kept replaying over and over. I had no idea what it meant, or why I was privileged to see this.

During breakfast the next day, from my spot on the parlor floor near the kitchen, I heard Gracie tell the family the story of how Jeb Crane had come late to the party at the fort and had told of seeing a large, silent group of carriages and horses traveling out past the fort to the old cemetery. So that's where they were going, I thought. I had felt that there was a destination they were all heading to, but I had no idea it was a cemetery. In fact, I did not even know there was a such a place nearby.

Gracie went on to tell how everyone had teased him and chided him about being drunk, because they were all sitting right there and had not seen it, but that he had insisted that he knew what he saw and even seemed a little spooked by it. Olinda and Lawrence exchanged knowing looks at one another all the while Gracie was telling the tale.

James had sat there, listening and laughing along with Gracie as she repeated the events of the night. He added that Jeb was such a wild character and known to enjoy his drink, so no one would believe anything he said anyway, and this story was no different. Gracie laughingly agreed with him.

Finally, Lawrence, whose weakened voice had nearly returned to normal now, related a story told to him many years ago by his grandfather. He told of a ghostly funeral procession that had been witnessed by two elderly ladies. As the story went, they were keeping watch over the body of the husband of one of the women. He had died earlier that day. The women sat in rocking chairs on the porch near the parlor where his body lay, and as they were sitting there late at night, they witnessed a strange procession by the light of the moon.

A group of carriages pulled by pairs of horses was traveling past the home, along with soldiers and others riding alongside. The lead carriage had one riderless horse for the dead soldier in the coffin on the bed of the wagon, or so they presumed. There was no sound coming from anything that they saw.

They claimed that they could see people in the carriages talking, with their heads moving as if in conversation. They could see the horses' hooves moving up and down as they marched, and the wheels of the carriages spinning, but there was no sound whatsoever coming from the whole line of mourners as they rode past. The group was heading down the road, making its way to the cemetery out near the old fort.

The next day—a Saturday—the women found that the only other witness was the caretaker of the woman's home, who saw the silent procession go past his cottage after he was awakened by the sound of a barking dog. They never did see the procession make its way back toward town. It was as if it had vanished into thin air.

This account had been passed down through generations, having taken place long, long ago. No one knew just who this dead soldier was or when the original funeral had taken place, only that these three people had witnessed it and that they had held to their story even on their deathbeds, swearing that it had truly happened. Lawrence said he had never heard of anyone witnessing this in his lifetime.

Gracie and James were dumbfounded. They could not believe what they had just heard. Maybe Jeb wasn't drunk after all, said Gracie. He would have nothing to gain by making it all up. Lawrence added that since yesterday had been a Friday, and the moon was very bright, maybe the funeral procession had been reenacted again.

As legend had it, this apparition could be seen on a Friday with a bright moon, but only three people would witness this strange sight. No one would know for certain, but I knew that the story Lawrence told was exactly what I had seen on the previous night. I had a lot of time to think about this, because as soon as their breakfast was completed, Olinda proceeded to launder me as she had said she would. As I hung on the clothesline to dry, I looked up into the trees and the sky for answers. I had no way to tell anyone about what I had seen in order to prove that another had seen the apparition. Granted, I am not human, but technically I have had sight since my awakening, and that in itself was a miracle.

I would have no answers that day and heard no more on the subject until a few weeks later, when Gracie said she heard that there *was* another person from town who had claimed to see the ghostly group that night. It was a young boy who had gone outside late at night to use the outhouse; he had seen the procession going past his home on its way to the fort. He had gone into the house crying to his parents, saying that they needed to get indoor plumbing, because he was never going outside at night to use the outhouse again!

So there it was—could I have been the third witness?

17

Summer quickly turned to autumn. The days, months, and years all seemed to be passing by so quickly. Before I knew it, Gracie had gone off to college and was back in Parrie again for the Christmas break. When she came home this time, she was with a young man named Charles. He was very courteous and well-mannered, and the family took to him right away.

Gracie had never brought a young man home from college before. She had, at one time or another, brought home local boys, most of whom were so smitten with her they barely spoke and could hardly take their eyes off her. But this one was different. He was very at ease with the family, a nice-looking fellow who seemed to win everyone over. That even included me, because Olinda had finally decided to mend some of my torn spots, so I was in her lap and I saw him when he came into the house with Gracie.

The two tumbled through the front door, laughing and talking, and shaking snowflakes out of their hair. Olinda stopped working on me and rose up to be introduced, as did Lawrence, who was sitting in a chair reading the newspaper. Shortly, James came home from his job at the newspaper office and joined the others as they settled around comfortably.

The young couple seemed so happy. One of them would start talking, and the other one would finish the sentence. Olinda and Lawrence glanced at one another and gave knowing smiles. Olinda asked how long they been seeing each other, and Gracie looked lovingly at Charles and said that they had first met at the beginning of her first semester at Clarkstown, but they had both been so busy with school and work that they hadn't caught up with one another at that point.

A few months ago though, they ended up working the same shift at the hospital. He was working an internship in the emergency room and delivered a patient to the surgical ward where she was working as an aide. The rest, as they say, was history. Apparently they had spent time together nearly every day since, whenever their studies and work shifts permitted.

Lawrence smiled at Olinda again. James, on the other hand, seemed oblivious, and he asked Charles a lot of questions about his hobbies and life outside school and work. Lawrence and Olinda were more curious about his studies and what major he had chosen. As it turned out, Charles was in his last year of medical school, with plans to become a family practice physician. This seemed to delight Olinda and Lawrence, both of whom wanted to find out more about this new young man's family and his hometown of Chicago.

Finally, Olinda set me aside on a chair in the corner of the room and asked Gracie to help her with meal preparations in the kitchen, so they would have a chance to talk. The men were in deep discussion about a problem Charles was having with his car, and Lawrence and James agreed to take a look at it with him in the morning when there was daylight.

That night, after enjoying the wonderful meal the women had prepared, the family introduced Charles to one of their favorite pastimes, playing euchre. He seemed to catch on very quickly. Olinda let James take her place for a while so she could pop a huge bowl of popcorn, and Lawrence got out a jug of homemade beer that he and his brother had made. A bit later, James took his leave, saying he had friends to meet up with. As he kissed Olinda's cheek when he was leaving, she told him to be careful—something she said to everyone when they left her home.

At the end of the night, Charles told the family that it had been a long time since he had this much fun letting loose. He had been keeping focused on his studies, he said, but then added with a smile that what little free time he had, he very much enjoyed spending it with Gracie.

Lawrence asked what else he enjoyed doing in his spare time, and Charles said he had enjoyed quail hunting with his father and uncles as a teenager, but that he did not have much time for it now. He commented that his father used to have a Brittany Spaniel that was a really good bird dog, but that it was long gone now. He also enjoyed golf, which was a game that Lawrence had never played. The two then talked about hunting for quite a while, with Charles saying that maybe he would have time for hunting again someday. Lawrence shared his own stories of hunting and fishing, which was another sport that Charles hadn't had much time for.

I could see and hear pretty well from where Olinda had left me in the corner, and I could tell that the family seemed to admire Charles. The best way to describe this was that, as I had heard people say before, they took to him like a duck to water. He seemed to fit in well with their small town ways, and given that he came from the city, Olinda and Lawrence were amazed. The few people they had come in contact with from Chicago had been stiff and unfriendly, but Charles seemed the total opposite. Having spent almost four years in the area for school, Charles had adapted to his surroundings well. He said he would be starting his residency in St. Louis next year after graduation, and had just received his acceptance letter.

At one point, Lawrence asked Charles where he planned to practice medicine after his residency was completed, and he said he would love to open a private practice in the southern Illinois area. He had fallen in love with the beauty of this part of the country while attending medical school here, and he said that although he would miss his family, he enjoyed the open spaces, compared to the confines of city living. He felt the people here were so much more down-to-earth. Charles told them that his mother had been from a rural area in Indiana, and so a lot of his love for small town life was probably passed down from her.

The next day, Gracie took Charles around to visit in the community. First they went to see Anna and Edward on the farm. Then they took a drive to see some of the places that were important to the family—to the quarry, out to the old fort, on to the river where Lawrence had piloted his tugboat, and finally past the house near there where her grandparents had lived and Lawrence had grown up. When they returned later in the day, they chattered on about all the places they had been. Charles said he felt like there was so much history in the area, it was almost as if these landmarks themselves could speak.

I heard all of this from my spot on the bed in Lawrence and Olinda's room, and I thought about what Charles had said. If only I could talk, I could tell him a story or two! Now that I was able to see, maybe I could start wishing for the ability to talk. However, I had a feeling that wouldn't happen.

Olinda invited Anna and Edward, Wallace and Felicity, and Albert and Caroline for dinner so the rest of the family could meet Charles. When they left that evening, everyone came into the bedroom to gather their coats, which had been laid on me during the visit. I heard Anna tell Olinda what a fine young man Charles seemed to be. She said that when they visited her and Edward earlier that day, the two of them seemed to get along so well and she hoped they would keep seeing one another, because she thought they were a good match. Olinda said she had to agree.

I myself felt that Charles seemed like a good man and I hoped he would treat Gracie well. I had come to love her very much, having watched her grow for even longer than I had Olinda. Gracie and James were both so special to me, and I hoped I would continue to see them and their future families for years to come.

Christmas came and went, and soon it was time for Gracie to go back to school. The house seemed much quieter after she was gone. James was gone so much with school and work that he was rarely home either.

At Easter, Gracie was busy working at the hospital and could not come home for a visit, so Olinda and

Lawrence spent the weekend visiting her and Charles down at Clarkstown. I wondered where they had gone when the house was so quiet for those few days.

I found out where they had been when Olinda called Anna to tell her about all they had seen and done while they were there. Olinda said it had done them good to get away, and to see the hospital where Gracie and Charles both worked. I did not hear the whole conversation, but it sounded like they had had a wonderful time and looked forward to seeing Gracie and Charles in a few months, when the semester ended.

Olinda was still very busy with her sewing, always making something for someone else. I heard her tell Lawrence one evening that when she finished her most recent commissioned piece, she felt it was time to start making a new quilt.

I heard this comment with deep sadness, as I knew my days comforting them were now numbered. Oh my, how this news upset me! Did I look that bad? I glanced at my cloth and noticed all the places she had patched me and mended holes and tears. I was no longer fluffy, and my edges were beginning to fray. It seemed that I was a mere shell of my former self.

I had spent so much time involved in my family's comings and goings lately that I had failed to pay attention to myself. Now it was too late, not that there was anything I could have done about it. Would I be relegated to some distant drawer or cupboard? Would I be shoved into a corner or on top of some old piece of unused furniture? I had a lot to think about that night as they settled down to sleep.

I wondered just how long it had taken Anna to complete me, and if I would be tossed aside like that old quilt I had spent time with in Evangeline's trunk. What had happened to it? I did not know, but I knew that I didn't want the same fate for myself. I thought of ways that I could still be useful, but then I realized I could not change her mind, even though I very much wanted to. My time here was limited, and I would do best not to dwell on it anymore.

I decided right then and there that I would enjoy what time I had with them until the day came that I was replaced with a new quilt, which I hoped would not be anytime too soon.

True to her word, the next day Olinda began going through the drawers of her chifforobe and boxes of cloth, sorting and cutting. I saw her bring in bags of new fabric and supplies that she had purchased. I realized this quilt would probably be even more beautiful than I was. It made me sad that I was going to see something put together that would push me out of their lives. There was nothing I could do but watch as she began sewing, working on the new quilt nearly every day.

As she got all the pieces sewed together, I could

see that they were in a different pattern than I was. It wasn't a beautiful fan, but pieces sewed in circles on cloth, very intricate and detailed—much different than I was, but still very lovely.

One day I heard her talking to Anna on the telephone, reporting just how far she had gotten on the quilt. Anna must have asked her what the pattern was, and Olinda said she was using a double wedding ring pattern. That made sense to me, because the circles resembled rings that were joined together. She said she was just about done piecing it, and then she would be ready to set up Evangeline's old quilt frame that had been stored in the cellar so she could start quilting it. Anna must have agreed to come and help her, because the two set up a date for the next week.

The day when Anna came to help Olinda put the new quilt in the frame came too soon for my liking. I remember it was a gloomy, rainy day; I heard raindrops at the window and saw them running down the glass panes. The outside weather matched my dreary mood.

Olinda commented that it had been so many years since she had had the time to quilt that she might have forgotten how. Anna told her it would all come back to her eventually; she just needed a little help getting started. The two rearranged furniture to make space in the parlor to set up the frame.

I could just see a small portion of it through the

open bedroom door, hopefully enough to monitor their progress. Once they had things all set up and ready to go, I realized that this could be helpful to me after all. For one thing, I had not been able to see myself being quilted. I could only hear Anna and Evangeline as they worked on my form. Maybe now that I could see, I would get some sort of closure as I saw this new quilt's progress, because I could imagine that they were once again working on me.

Much as I tried to watch though, I mostly saw their backs as they bent over the quilt and talked to one another while working on my replacement. My mind was troubled, and I could not concentrate on the words they were speaking. I felt like I was in another world entirely. I thought of all the things that might drag out the completion of this quilt—such as the quilt turning out poorly or Olinda deciding not to use it—but none of them was anything I truly wished would happen.

My desire for this family was always one of true happiness, and if this is what Olinda wanted, I had to learn to accept my fate and have only good thoughts.

Toward lunchtime, they took a break. As they got up from their chairs, I strained to see what I could, but it was hopeless. I was too far away to see anything but the backs of the chairs and the wooden frame. This was of no help to me whatsoever. When they came back to begin working again, I tried to make out their conversation, but the two spoke softly to one another and I couldn't make out their words. Such was my situation for that day and many days thereafter.

I did hear one announcement as Anna left one day: She said she would not be back the next day, because Edward had a doctor's appointment in Robertsville, and she wanted to go with him. Olinda told her not to worry, that she had some things to get done as well, and she would work on the new quilt as she had time.

She said she hoped to have it done in a few weeks though, because it took up too much room in the parlor. That apparently, would add to my undoing. Where Anna had had a space to work on me where I was out of the family's way, Olinda did not have that luxury. Her house was set up differently, without that large front room. Oh, how I wished I was back in Anna's front room, starting my time here all over again! What I wouldn't give to be brand new and useful once more. How many experiences would this new quilt have? I hoped not as many as I had had, and I prayed it would not get to see and hear things like I was able to.

Sure enough, within a few short weeks, the time came to take the new quilt out of the frame. I was amazed at how quickly the two women had completed the new quilt. I knew there was urgency to get it done and out of the way in the parlor, but yet I could not know how it would affect me until it happened.

Once again, just like Anna and Evangeline had done before, Anna and Olinda placed the new quilt on the bed so they could hem the edges. And I could see absolutely nothing, because the new quilt had been laid on top of me. Oh, how I hated that! It felt so nice and new and fluffy! The word that came to mind was one I had heard long ago, and I think it was what I was feeling: jealousy. That had to be it. I was jealous of this quilt for being new and pretty and replacing me where I had been for so long.

The two women worked on opposite sides of the bed, but since my vision was blocked, I could not see their progress. I not only wanted to see how far they had gotten, I wanted to see the completed project. I wanted to get one last good look at it before they took me off and laid this quilt on Lawrence and Olinda's bed, thereby committing me to some forgotten place.

When they finished, they proceeded to fold the quilt back a little, and I could finally see what it looked like fully completed. It was beautiful! There were no other words to describe it. I have to admit that it was probably more gorgeous than I ever was. I had to give Anna and Olinda a lot of credit for creating such a lovely work of art.

My rival was more than I expected, and this realization hurt me deeply. The rings intertwined with each other, each one a work of art in itself. The pieces of cloth were stitched together in a burst of colored patterns, and the rest of it was snowy white fabric throughout. It made my dingy self feel ashamed of my appearance. As I gazed at the new quilt, I realized that if I had to be replaced, at least it was by something as wondrous as this—not some simple, hastily made coverlet.

But then, something unexpected happened. Olinda continued to fold the quilt, and she and Anna put it into a fresh pillowcase. I watched intently as Olinda placed it high up on top of the chifforobe, saying that that would be a good spot for now. What was happening? Why wasn't she putting it on the bed and replacing me? They left the room, and sometime later Anna left the house, after she had helped Olinda take down the frame and rearrange the furniture.

I was at my wit's end trying to figure out what was going on. Was this a surprise for Lawrence? No, that could not be, because he had seen the quilt taking shape as they worked, and he knew what it looked like. I could not figure out why Olinda would make this new quilt, only to set it aside once it was completed. I could think of no logical explanation and was most puzzled by this turn of events.

18

Springtime had arrived—I could feel it coming in through the open windows. I could hear the birds chirping, and there was often a soft breeze rustling the curtains hanging at Olinda and Lawrence's bedroom windows. Outside the window closest to me, I could see new leaves on the tree alongside the house. This confirmed to me what Lawrence had once said: Spring had sprung.

Over the past few days, I had continued to wonder about the new quilt on top of the chifforobe. It sat there quietly, and no one moved it. For the life of me, I was still puzzled as to Olinda's intent for it. I had overcome my initial hate of the lovely masterpiece, and I actually felt somewhat sorry for it. Would no one see its beauty? Would it be relegated to the top of the chifforobe for years, just as I had rested on the quilt rack, waiting to be used?

Maybe my time here was not done yet, and Olinda was just planning for when I got to be totally useless. As time passed, that was the conclusion I came to. I was still suitable for use, but maybe this new quilt was to be used only for special occasions, like I had been originally—when company came, for example.

It would be several more months before I realized what was going on.

With the coming of spring, there was another wash day for me. It seemed that I was forever getting dirty, or maybe Olinda was trying to wear me out before she put the new quilt on the bed. Either way, I was in a strange mood as I hung on the clothesline the day Gracie came home for summer break. Charles had brought her, because I saw her get out of his car. I should have been excited to see her, but I was forlorn and feeling sorry for myself. I was embarrassed, too, as they looked over at me while they sat on the back porch waiting for Olinda to come home from the post office.

I heard Gracie telling Charles about the day she got into trouble smearing jelly all over me. He laughed at the story, as did she. She said that she barely remembered the incident, but her parents had told her what had happened. She remembered the paddling she received though! She went on to say that I had been such a lovely quilt when she was a child.

Oh, yes, I thought, rub it in! I was magnificent at one time, but at least I was still useful! I didn't blame her for saying these things—she was just stating facts. Wait until you see my substitute, I brooded, you will really feel sorry for me then.

Olinda returned shortly and, giving them each a big hug, she took a seat on one of the chairs scattered around on the porch. Olinda said that Lawrence would be home soon, so while they waited for him to come home, they caught up on news. Lawrence and Albert had just completed a project at the cabinet shop, and Lawrence had told her that he expected to be home early that afternoon after delivering it. As if on cue, Lawrence's old truck pulled into the driveway, and he joined the others.

There was a feeling of anticipation in the air—something I could not quite figure out. I noticed that Olinda and Lawrence kept smiling at the couple a lot, and I assumed it was because they were glad to have them home, especially their daughter. Gracie chattered on about how she would be finished with her studies in just one more semester. She had studied and worked hard the past year so she could get her nursing degree early. Lawrence told her that he and Olinda were both very proud of her. They also wished her a belated happy birthday, for she had turned 20 years old just a few days earlier. My, how those years had flown! It seemed to me that Gracie had just been born.

Gracie had turned out to be such a beautiful young woman, and James a fine young man as well. I think I felt as proud of them as Olinda and Lawrence must have been. James would have only one more year of high school, and soon he would be making his way in the world just like Gracie was.

All this time, Charles seemed to be very preoccupied with his own thoughts, not really joining in the conversation, just rubbing his hands up and down his knees and shifting in his seat. There was a moment of awkward silence, and then all of a sudden Charles told Gracie that he'd like to ask her an important question. Then he quickly got down on one knee in front of her, reached in his pocket, and produced a small box. Gracie's hands flew to her mouth as he opened it! I glanced from Lawrence to Olinda, and I saw them beaming with pride.

The next words out of Charles' mouth were asking if Gracie would do him the honor of becoming his wife. He took something out of the box, and I could see the sun glinting off the diamond ring he held in his hand. Of course, she said yes! The two hugged and kissed, and he slid the ring onto her finger—it fit perfectly. Gracie grabbed Charles around the neck and they hugged and kissed again. Then Olinda and Lawrence stood up and they all hugged each other—smiling, laughing, and with Olinda and Gracie crying at the same time.

I was overjoyed for them as well! What great news! This excitement made me forget my circumstances momentarily, and I reveled in the joy of the announcement.

Gracie couldn't take her eyes off the beautiful ring. After Lawrence and Olinda went into the house so the young couple could have some privacy, Charles and Gracie spoke quietly as she rested her head upon his shoulder. When she told him he had done a wonderful job of picking out the perfect ring for her, he told her how happy he was that she liked it. Then she told him she didn't like it, she loved it! That brought a huge smile to Charles' face.

Gracie mentioned that she didn't think her parents seemed very surprised, and Charles told her that he had already asked their permission, and they had given him their blessing. He had talked with Lawrence and Olinda over Easter break when they visited Gracie and Charles at school. Did she remember when he had taken them out to supper at one of the restaurants in Clarkstown that weekend? She said she did remember when he had taken her parents out to supper while she worked, and at the time she thought it was such a thoughtful thing for him to have done. She now realized that he had an ulterior motive!

He winked at her and said even though they had only been dating for the past nine months, he knew from the moment he saw her—that first day they met at the hospital a year and a half ago—that she was the one for him.

They sat there a while longer, holding hands as Gracie admired the ring. They were still sitting there talking when James came home, and they shared their news with him. My goodness, he whooped and hollered and carried on! He was so excited and happy for them, and he said that now he would get the brother he had always wanted. He congratulated them both, pumping Charles' hand up and down and giving Gracie a slobbery kiss on the cheek and a quick hug.

As they all sat on the porch talking, oblivious to me, I thought about the fact that, once I was replaced, I would not be a witness to these everyday events. I felt very distraught, reflecting on that realization. Shortly after, Olinda came to retrieve me and placed me back on the bed. I felt fresher, but still unsettled about my future.

The next day was Mother's Day, and they all enjoyed celebrating both the holiday and the engagement. The next week, the family had plans to attend Charles' medical school graduation and would be meeting his parents for the first time. Before they left that morning, Lawrence asked Olinda if Gracie had mentioned when the wedding would take place. Olinda said that Gracie had not talked about a specific date yet, but maybe the subject would come up today—perhaps when they went out for lunch after the commencement.

Lawrence replied that if the wedding was to be this summer before Charles went to St. Louis to begin his residency, as he had told them at Easter, they would need to choose a date soon. Because Gracie had mentioned wanting a small family wedding—nothing fancy—Olinda thought it wouldn't be a problem to make plans for a wedding just a few months away.

Lawrence said he hoped that Gracie would still finish her last semester of nursing school, since she was so close to being done, but Olinda assured him that Gracie was certain she would have no trouble transferring to another school.

Then she said something that was puzzling to me. She told Lawrence that she was just glad to have their gift out of the way. I didn't know what to make of that. What gift did they plan to give Gracie and Charles? I had no idea at all what Olinda was hinting at. I pondered this for a while, but finally gave up because I could not imagine what gift Olinda was referring to.

As it turned out, Charles was needed in St. Louis ahead of schedule, and he left several days after his graduation. In the meantime, Gracie would be staying at home in Parrie until the wedding, working at her old job at the hospital in Robertsville. Gracie cried and cried the night before he left. He assured her that they would be married soon, but until then they would get together on weekends whenever they could.

She missed him so much! The two talked on the phone every Thursday evening to discuss their weekend plans—whether Charles would be able to come back to Parrie, or whether Gracie would catch a bus to St. Louis on Friday after work. Some weekends they were not able to see each other at all, with their crazy work schedules, but more often than not, either Gracie went to the city, or Charles came to Parrie.

One weekend, Charles came to visit, and they all sat down to plan the wedding. Earlier that day, the couple had visited with the new priest assigned to St. Joseph's, Father Bowen. He told them that he needed four weeks to post their banns to the marriage tribunal with the diocese, and since it was now the end of June, the earliest Saturday they could choose was August 2nd.

Gracie did not want to wait any longer than that, because she had already made arrangements to complete the last semester of her nursing studies at the same university where Charles was doing his residency at the hospital. Her classes were to start the second week of August, so if Charles could get away, they might be able to have a short honeymoon.

One evening, when Gracie came home from working at the hospital, she and Olinda sat in the parlor, and I heard them making lists of things to be ordered or bought for the wedding. True to her word, Gracie said that she wanted no big fuss. All she wanted was to be Charles' bride and to begin her life in St. Louis with her husband. Olinda said that since Gracie was a small town girl, she hoped that big city life would suit her. Gracie replied she didn't care where they lived, just as long as she and Charles were together.

Gracie and Olinda worked on the short guest list, mostly family and a few of Gracie's closest friends, along with a few of Olinda and Lawrence's. She had gotten a list from Charles with names of the family members and school buddies he wanted to invite. Olinda was worried about where the out-of-towners would sleep, but Gracie said that more than likely, they planned to stay in a hotel in St. Louis and then drive to Parrie on the morning of the wedding.

For this reason, Gracie wanted only a small reception instead of a big meal: small sandwiches, cake, punch, and coffee served at the church hall. Olinda said that she had never heard of such a thing, not having a big meal for the guests! But Gracie assured her that that was the way all big city weddings were nowadays. Olinda was disappointed, but she went along with Gracie's choices. The wedding would be at ten o'clock in the morning, with a light luncheon afterward, some time for visiting and opening gifts, and then all would be done by midafternoon.

Olinda asked about music and dancing, but Gracie only frowned and said they didn't want that. Upon hearing Olinda's dismay at the thought of no music, Gracie said that, if anything, she would ask the church organist to play light background music on the piano in the hall during the reception. Gracie said she had already asked Shirley to be her maid of honor, and Charles had asked his good friend Bob to be his best man. That was to be the extent of the wedding party. She planned to ask James to be an usher and seat the guests at church, and ask Charles' twin sisters, Betty and Bonnie, who were his only siblings, to serve the cake and punch.

As for the rest of the details, Gracie had already bought a few decorations, and she had ordered bouquets, corsages, and boutonnieres for the wedding party and their parents from the new florist in Robertsville. The florist was also allowing her to rent potted plants and ferns for decorations.

Gracie planned on wearing a light pink summer suit for the wedding—one she had bought just last week when shopping with Shirley. It was something she could wear again if she wanted to. Olinda's mouth popped open at that, and she asked if Gracie was sure she didn't want to wear an actual wedding dress. Although the suit was indeed practical, Olinda wondered aloud if Gracie might someday regret not having a wedding gown for her special day. But Gracie had her mind made up, and so that was the end of that.

Olinda told Gracie that she and Lawrence had saved some money over the years for her wedding, although she had to admit that this wedding was not going to cost them very much. Gracie told her that with Lawrence having been ill and the struggles they had had over the years, it was never her intention to cause further financial hardship for her parents, and that this small wedding was her choice.

Olinda cried softly, telling Gracie that she should not feel that way, that it was their right to give her a nice wedding and that they would make it work. But Gracie replied that a simple wedding was all she ever really wanted, and she hoped that Olinda and Lawrence understood, with no hard feelings on their part. Gracie told Olinda that if they wanted to help them out with the cake or food, that would be more than enough. Olinda hugged Gracie and told her if that was truly her wish, then they would go along with it.

Olinda confessed to Gracie just how much she would miss her. Gracie hugged her mother and said that she would miss her, too, but she assured her mother that they would be able to visit often and that they would talk every week on the telephone, just like she and Charles were doing now.

The remaining weeks flew by. On the day before the wedding, Gracie took Olinda shopping to buy a dress for the occasion. When they came home, she brought the dress into the bedroom and hung it on the hook behind the door. It was a lovely shade of what I learned was green (very much like the color of Anna and Gracie's eyes).

Once the door was closed, she took down the folded quilt—my replacement—from the top of the chifforobe, where it had been waiting for these past few months. I knew it! Here it comes now, I thought. She would take me off the bed and put this new quilt on, because company was coming for the wedding, and she was ashamed of me. The day had finally come to retire this old rag!

At least that is what I thought was going to happen. But, lo and behold, Olinda gathered some soft paper and began to wrap up the quilt. Oh, my goodness! What was going on?

So many thoughts went through my mind, but then it finally dawned on me that this lovely new quilt was not a replacement for me, but a wedding present for Gracie and Charles! This was the gift that Olinda had gotten out of the way! No wonder she had rushed to get it done! She wanted it gone from the parlor and out of the way before Gracie came home to see her working on it. My guess was that after their Easter visit to Clarkstown, when Charles had asked them for Gracie's hand and told them his intention to be married before the end of the summer, Olinda had decided to make this new quilt for their wedding gift. She would have known that she had to get it done in a short amount of time. I was so overjoyed at this news! I was not going to be replaced after all!

I watched her as she wrapped it and tied it with a pale blue ribbon. A few silent tears rolled down her cheeks, but as she wiped them away, she was smiling. I guessed that she was crying tears of joy for her baby girl, who was taking this big step toward a new life with Charles. I only wished that I could be there the next day to join them, like I had been at the wedding of Olinda and Lawrence, but I knew this would not happen. All I could do was imagine how lovely it would all be and wait to see if I would hear anything about it from the family after it was over.

The next day, they all prepared to leave the house, and Olinda came into the bedroom right before they left to retrieve the wrapped package. I would have loved to see Gracie's reaction when she and Charles opened it, because I am sure they would realize how much love had gone into the making of it, not only her mother's, but her grandmother's as well.

Olinda looked radiant in her green dress and Lawrence handsome in his rented suit. Since his illness, his own suit was much too big on him, and it was also too out of style for the occasion. I only saw a fleeting glimpse of Gracie in her pink suit as she passed down the hallway and out the door of the house. I realized that this would probably be the last time I would see her for a very long time. Then the family all left for the wedding.

It was much, much later when they returned. As Olinda came into the bedroom, she commented to Lawrence that even though it had not been as long a day as when they married, she was tired enough from all the festivities. He chuckled and said they were a bit older now than they were on that long ago day. He admitted, too, that he was worn out and felt like he needed a nap.

When James came home a bit later, I finally heard the three of them talking about the wedding. I listened with rapt attention. It sounded as if everything had gone well, and all the guests had remarked on what a wonderful gathering it was. Olinda said she need not have worried about what others thought of the simple affair, as they all thought it was quite tasteful—from the small tea sandwiches to the beautiful and delicious cake.

I heard Olinda say that, despite her initial apprehension about Gracie's plans for an unconventional wedding, she had apparently known what she was doing. Everything had turned out well—very elegant and sophisticated—something unusual for weddings in Parrie. Those usually had too much drinking and dancing, and too much carrying on into the late hours. Minnie's parents, Adele and John, were there. They had attended many weddings since moving to the city, and they had remarked that it reminded them of an elegant garden party, even though it was held indoors to escape the Midwestern August heat.

Lawrence mentioned that he thought Charles' parents, Millie and Jack, were appreciative of the hospitality they were shown by everyone in the family, and that he and Jack had had a nice visit over coffee and cake at the reception. Olinda had chatted with Millie while they admired the gifts the newlyweds had unwrapped—including a set of china from the groom's parents. There were also many cards that Gracie and Charles had chosen to open later, when they were at home alone.

Olinda mentioned that she was thrilled that Gracie and Charles seemed to love the quilt and that they said that the double wedding ring pattern was a clever choice. Gracie had apparently thanked her mother and Anna profusely for the fantastic work they had done on the quilt and said there was not another quilt as beautiful as this one in all the world. Gracie told them she could not wait to put it on the bed at their apartment.

Olinda told Lawrence about another part of her conversation with Millie. Millie had apparently told Olinda that she had never seen such a stunning work of art. She said that she might even want to have a quilt made in a different pattern, and offered to pay

Olinda to make one for her someday, since she herself knew nothing about quilting.

I also found out another piece of news. Apparently, James had a girlfriend, and he had taken her with him to the wedding. Her name was Patricia, and Olinda and Lawrence had only met her a few times. Her family had moved to town when her father took over as the new president of the bank after Minnie's parents moved away.

Patricia was a year older than James. She had just graduated from high school in the spring and was already working at the bank as a teller. That must be where James had met her, when he took a cash deposit from the newspaper office one day. As the three sat quietly talking, Olinda and Lawrence told James that they thought she was a lovely girl and that he needed to bring her home so they could get better acquainted.

Since the subject had been brought up about banking, Olinda chose this time to mention the savings account she had started for James when he was still a young boy. He told her that he already knew about it, although he was very surprised to hear that they were his benefactors. He revealed that he had found out about it just the day before, when he went to open an account.

Apparently, all this time James had been cashing his checks and keeping all his money in a box under his bed so he would have it when he wanted or needed it. A few days ago, he had mentioned to Patricia that he did this, and she convinced him that it would be safer to put it in the bank—plus the money would earn interest there.

When he approached her about it yesterday at the bank, she checked their files and said it was not necessary to start a new account, because he already had one. James was surprised and told her there must be some mistake, but she confirmed that there was already an account in his name. There was a co-signer on the account, and that person held the passbook. Patricia said that she couldn't disclose any additional information without consent from the main account holder, unless he had the passbook with him.

James told her that he did not have it and, in fact, he had not even known such an account existed. She told him to find out who his benefactor was, suggesting to him it was probably his parents. James said he told her he did not think that was the case, but he thought he knew just who it might be.

Olinda then came into the bedroom, took a small book out of the dresser drawer, and went back into the parlor to give it to James. He must have opened it, and then he let out a slow whistle. Apparently, it was a pretty nice sum, because James seemed to be dumbfounded. He exclaimed that he could not believe there was that much money already saved! James thanked his parents over and over again for doing that for him; he obviously had no idea they had done this. He said that he had assumed that his grandparents, Anna and Edward, had started the account for all the times he had helped at the farm. He had planned to ask them about it today after the wedding, but hadn't had an opportunity to do so.

Olinda assured him that she had done this because he had so generously turned over his paper route money to help them out when Lawrence was sick and could not work. She felt it was not right to take money from their son, so she had only kept a small amount from his earnings and had put the rest in the bank. When times were better, once Lawrence had recovered and was working again, she paid back all she had borrowed, depositing it into the account with interest added.

He thanked them profusely and said he would keep adding to it; he promised that what little he spent, he would spend wisely. His intent was to save up enough to buy a car. He told them that there was nearly enough in the account now, and with his next several paychecks, he should be able to get the one he had his eye on.

James added that right now there was enough for a motorcycle, but Lawrence balked at that idea, saying he felt they were unsafe and hoped that James would not spend his hard earned money on one. Apparently, Lawrence had witnessed a horrible motor-cycle accident along the highway coming into Parrie. A young man had hit an oncoming truck and was killed instantly. Lawrence told James how helpless he had felt at the time, since he came upon the crash just after it happened. It was a scene he said he could never forget.

Lawrence also felt that a motorcycle would simply be a poor choice, and that a car would be more practical for year-round use. James said he had to agree, that with all the cold weather and snow they had every winter, a car would definitely be a better choice for him.

I listened as their conversation wound down and they headed into the dining room to eat a light supper of wedding leftovers. Later that night, when Olinda and Lawrence were getting ready for bed, Lawrence told Olinda how proud he was of her for taking the initiative to start the account for James. He said that he knew that at the time she had done it, she had only James' best interests in mind, and he felt that paying back the money they had used was a wise and noble decision. He said he always hated being in debt to anyone, especially his own son.

Olinda said it had never crossed her mind to keep any of the money, and they had only used it out of necessity at the time. She said that she had felt a huge weight lift off her shoulders when she was able to pay back every last dime. She was glad the subject was out in the open, because she had been looking for the right time to give the passbook to James, and now the opportunity seemed to have presented itself in just the right way.

As the two drifted off to sleep, I realized what a loving act Olinda had performed. She seemed to be such a selfless person, always doing for others, and working so hard to give her family all they needed. She was a lot like her parents, because Anna and Edward were the same way, helping out their children whenever they got in a bind, never expecting anything in return. I realized then that of all the families in all of Parrie and beyond, I sure fell into a good one when Anna chose to create me that long ago day.

That fall, Olinda and Lawrence saw Gracie and Charles several times. A few weeks after the wedding, they traveled to St. Louis to visit them at their home: Gracie and Charles lived in the top floor apartment of a house owned by a friendly older couple. The newlyweds returned to Parrie one day in late September so they could be with the whole family when they picked apples and made apple butter at the farm, a tradition the family had held dear for many, many years.

As Gracie had promised, Olinda and Gracie talked on the telephone weekly. Every Thursday evening I listened in on the one-sided conversation, which always ended with Olinda saying, "I love you, too." She often got tearful after these calls, and she would tell Lawrence just how much she missed her Gracie.

He would always remind her that their daughter was a grown woman and that she had her own life to live now. Still, Olinda said, it hurt so much. Lawrence mentioned that Gracie had been gone much longer periods of time when she was away at school, but Olinda said it wasn't the same, because she had known then that Gracie would always come back home. Now Gracie was gone for good and would not be returning.

It was about that time that Olinda began to realize just how very little time James was spending at home. She worried about him spending so much time at Patricia's on school nights. Finally, one day she mentioned this to Lawrence. He said the best way to find out would be just to ask James himself about all his comings and goings, when he would be home, how long he would be gone, and where he was heading.

James usually told her everything, but lately he had been vague, and oftentimes he would say he wasn't sure himself when he would be home. He was either heading out with his buddies, working at the newspaper, or going over to Patricia's to visit with her. It seemed that lately he was there more often than not. The fact was, Lawrence and Olinda had still not been able to spend any time with the young girl, and Olinda felt that it was very important for them to do just that. She asked James about a good time for a visit, but he always brushed her off. He said that he would ask Patricia and report back, but he never did.

Finally, after repeatedly telling James that they would very much like to visit with Patricia, but getting only vague responses in reply, Olinda apparently took the matter into her own hands. I heard her tell Lawrence one night that she had gone to the bank and talked with Patricia. Olinda told her that they would very much like it if she could come for supper on Sunday evening. Patricia was happy to accept, saying she had no other plans. She said she would tell James first thing that evening when he came over.

Olinda told Lawrence about it that night as they got ready for bed, and said that maybe they would finally get to have a nice sit-down visit with them. She felt that James was home so rarely, it was almost like he didn't live there at all. It seemed like he only slept and ate breakfast at the house, because he often stayed late at the newspaper office and then would head to Patricia's house to join her family for supper most nights. He usually came in late at night after they were in bed. Olinda felt her son was slipping through her fingers, just as Gracie had. He was much too young for this, still a school boy, and she did not like it, she told Lawrence.

The next night, James came home earlier than usual and sat at the desk in the parlor with his schoolbooks open. Olinda and Lawrence took this opportunity to ask a few questions. First, Olinda asked him if Patricia had spoken to him about Sunday, and he said that she had. After a few more questions about how things were going with his job and school, since they rarely saw him anymore, James hung his head and finally admitted to his parents just what was going on.

He said that he had been doing poorly in his chemistry class and that Patricia was helping him with his school work. He said he had been having trouble ever since the beginning of his senior year, and he did not want to let on to them just what was happening, because he was ashamed. Olinda and Lawrence told him that he should never feel that he could not talk to them about his problems. He admitted that he had also not wanted to tell them for fear they would make him quit his job at the newspaper.

Patricia had been so nice in helping him, he said, and he was actually doing better now. Studying with her, his grades had improved a great deal, and without her assistance, he had been worried he would not pass the class. After all, he said, this was his last year, and he would have no chance to make it up. He mentioned being concerned that if he didn't get better grades, he would not be able to attend college to get a journalism degree, which was something he had wanted to do ever since he started working at the newspaper.

Olinda and Lawrence were surprised to hear all this. James had always been an above-average student, and he had never had any problems with his schoolwork in the past. They seemed at a loss for words, unsure what to say about it, but they expressed gratefulness for Patricia taking the time to help him.

Patricia had decided not to go to college to pursue a teaching degree and had started the job at the bank, James said. But then she realized just how much she enjoyed helping him, and she had now decided to enroll next year after all, so maybe some good had come from him needing help. If he could pass this class and graduate, they would end up starting their freshmen year together. Olinda and Lawrence told James that the next time something like this was going on, he shouldn't keep them in the dark about his troubles. He agreed that it was foolish of him to do so, and he promised to keep them informed from then on.

Olinda decided to make her specialty, chicken and dumplings, for Sunday. She spent the afternoon cooking her chicken, cleaning all the meat off the bones and rolling out her dumplings; she also baked a cake. Olinda was just finishing cleaning up when James arrived with Patricia.

James brought Patricia into the parlor, and Olinda and Lawrence joined them. From what I could see, Patricia appeared to be a lovely girl—not as slim as Gracie, and nearly as tall as James. She had hair the color of the sun, and she wore it pulled back with combs of some sort. With James' dark hair and coloring in contrast, the pair made a handsome couple.

Olinda served glasses of iced tea as they asked Patricia about her job and her family. She told them that the job was going well, but that she thought James might have shared with them that she would be going to the university next year to pursue a teaching degree. She had put it off for a year, because she had been undecided, and her father had said there was no rush. He figured that she could work for a year if she wanted to see if she preferred banking, and she might even choose to major in business instead, like he had. She reiterated that helping James with his chemistry lessons had reinstilled the desire to move forward with education, and she was looking forward to it.

Patricia told them about her two younger brothers, one in his second year of high school and the other one in the eighth grade. Her mother was a housewife, and her father, as they knew, was the new bank president. She said that so far they liked Parrie even though small town living was much different than living in the city. They continued with small talk about the weather, Gracie and Charles' recent wedding, and other news around the town.

At one point in the conversation, Patricia shared that her parents had just purchased a television set the day before, something Lawrence and Olinda had heard about but had not yet been able to see in person. Lawrence said they had been to the moving picture show at the Parrie theater earlier this year, and they had seen something about this. There was a short film reel advertising this new device before they showed the feature film.

Patricia went on to say how much her father enjoyed it, especially since he could now watch St. Louis news coverage rather than just listen to it on the radio. Since St. Louis is where Patricia's family had moved from, her mother enjoyed being able to keep up with what was going on back in their old hometown. She said her father felt it was important to be informed about what was happening in our country and beyond, especially after the recent war. She added that they also enjoyed some of the broadcasts that were being shown from other parts of the country, such as New York and Hollywood, California.

James added that the television programs were really something to see, and he hoped Olinda and Lawrence would be able to get a television set someday, too. Lawrence doubted they would get one anytime soon, and he told James that he was lucky he could view one at Patricia's house.

Soon the family went into the dining room, and I could not see them or hear much after that. I was only able to make out bits and pieces. I heard them laughing and talking, but I could not make out anything they were saying. I patiently waited for them to come back into the parlor, but they didn't return until much later and by then, James and Patricia were heading out the door so he could take her home.

Apparently, they had enjoyed a new board game that James bought at the variety store in Robertsville. The two couples had passed the evening playing the new game, listening to the radio, and talking. As Patricia was going through the doorway, she turned around and thanked Olinda for the lovely meal. She said she would pass the recipe for the Jell-O salad on to her mother, because she had liked it so much and she knew that her mother would, too. She also said she hoped Lawrence and Olinda could attend the party at her home on Friday, because her parents were looking forward to meeting them.

When Lawrence and Olinda retired for the night, shortly after James returned home, Olinda said she was looking forward to meeting Patricia's family and friends on Friday night at the party in honor of Patricia's 18th birthday. Patricia had said that since it was close to Halloween, they had considered making it a costume party, but then they decided against it, mostly because her father thought it was silly for adults to dress up.

As they lay in bed, Lawrence said he had to agree with Patricia's father on that front. Olinda chuckled and said they probably wouldn't have known what to wear, had they been asked to wear costumes, and they both laughed as she suggested dressing up as a couple of clowns or hobos.

For some reason, this reminded her of a story

Anna had told her about a couple in town who had dated for many years, but the man would not commit to marriage. The people in Parrie most certainly did not approve of this situation. Olinda said that a few of his friends and other locals had dressed up in crazy costumes so that no one would know their identity. In the wee hours of the night, they went to the man's house to hold a shivaree, loudly banging on pots and pans and ringing bells. The group continued carrying on like this at the young fellow's doorstep, pounding on his front door and shouting to him that he needed to make an honest woman out of his girl. They caused such a ruckus that he finally came out and told them all to go home.

Shortly after that, the couple did get married and, as they say, lived happily ever after. No one knew if it was the shivaree that had finally led him to ask for her hand, or if he would have married her anyway, even without their help. Lawrence laughed and told Olinda that he had never heard that story. Since his family had always lived out near the river, he did not know all the goings on in town like her family did when they lived in town so many years ago.

The couple reminisced about their younger days and about how things had changed, the relatively new invention of the television, and how much the world itself had changed since they were children.

Lawrence said he wondered what the world would be like in another 50 years. Olinda said that they probably wouldn't be around to find out, because in 50 years she would be 93 and he would be 96.

Olinda said she had always hoped that, since she was born the year of the St. Louis World's Fair, maybe someday it would be held in St. Louis again and she would like to go to it. Lawrence promised her that if it was ever held in St. Louis in their lifetime, he would make sure she got to attend.

They kissed one another, and soon it became quiet. I realized that they had finally drifted off to sleep. This was by far my favorite time of day—when Olinda and Lawrence had these conversations before falling asleep. It was all so intimate, and I felt so much more a part of their lives each time it occurred.

The next week went by quickly, and Olinda and Lawrence left the house early Friday evening to head to the party. When they returned, Olinda couldn't stop talking about it. She chattered on and on about Patricia's parents and their home. It was a home that Olinda had been in many times when she was younger. Minnie's parents, John and Adele, had lived in the house before they moved to Bayerville to be nearer Minnie, after she and George moved there for his job. Olinda said she could not get over how Patricia's parents had updated the house, and just how different it looked inside.

There were two other couples from St. Louis who drove down for the party, too. Patricia's aunt and uncle came to help celebrate her birthday, and so did some good friends of the family, the parents of one of Patricia's friends from childhood. Olinda mentioned how curious it was that Patricia's father was now the bank president, and Minnie's father had also had that role in town before his move to Bayerville. The house must attract bankers, she said, for it was quite an imposing home in Parrie.

From Olinda's comparing the evening's events with Lawrence, I gathered that the women had spent time in the parlor visiting and chatting, while the men played cards and smoked cigars in the den across the hall.

Olinda said the women were very friendly; they had exchanged favorite recipes, and Trudy, Patricia's mother, had thanked Olinda for the Jell-O salad recipe she had given Patricia the week before. Trudy must have made it for the party, and it seemed that it had turned out to be a crowd pleaser. Olinda seemed happy about that. She talked about other tasty dishes at the party, too, including the delicious chocolate cake from the bakery in town.

Later on, Patricia had requested that music be left on the radio for the younger crowd to dance to on the back patio, since the weather was unseasonably warm for the end of October. The radio cabinet had been moved to the kitchen so the younger ones could hear it better outside.

When the men took a break from their card game, the adults all had a chance to see the television set that James had spoken so much of. They had all gathered around it in the den, and then Patricia's father, Bill, turned it on for them so he could show them how it worked. It apparently took some time to warm up, and one fellow commented that it might be broken already, but Bill assured them that it didn't come on immediately. The picture tube was slow to respond, but sure enough, it finally worked.

Everyone must have gathered around the small screen, which was set into a large Bakelite cabinet. One of the men commented that the screen should be bigger for the size of the box it was in. Bill adjusted the tuner, and everyone was amazed when they were able to see an episode of a show called *The World in Your Home.* The show was almost over, and soon there were commercial breaks, just like on radio shows, except that these commercials could not only be heard, but seen—advertising things such as Goodyear tires and Chiquita bananas.

After that, a show came on with a woman demonstrating how to arrange furniture in your home. The women paid attention to that for a while, and the men went back to their card game. Olinda told Lawrence that after the men left, she had seen advertisements for the Ajax foaming cleanser that she regularly used. She said it was funny to see these commercials after hearing them on the radio for so long. Olinda also said that one of the women asked Trudy how she liked the picture box, and Trudy said it was alright, that she didn't watch it much, but that Bill seemed pleased with it.

As they got ready for bed, Olinda told Lawrence that the decorating show seemed kind of silly to her. Why would they film somebody arranging chairs and tables, when everybody's home was set up differently? How many people would be interested in a show like that? She didn't understand the fascination.

Lawrence told her that he had no answer, but that he believed it would be a long time before they purchased such a contraption. Olinda said that was fine with her. It might be nice for some people, but she liked her radio and she did not need to see people arranging furniture or advertisements for the things she bought. If they chose to, she and Lawrence could just visit the movie theater in town like they always had.

I thought this television machine sounded interesting. I, too, had been listening to the radio for many years, as long as Olinda had, in fact—and to the phonograph at Anna and Edward's before that. I enjoyed the music very much, but I felt that being able to see these moving images as she had described them would help my days pass more quickly when nothing of interest was happening in the house. But I had a feeling that if Olinda and Lawrence ever did buy one of those devices, it would probably be out of my line of vision anyway, and so it wouldn't be any different than hearing the radio.

20

One day in early spring about a year and a half later, my day of reckoning finally came. I cannot say that it was a complete surprise, after my misunderstanding about the quilt for Gracie and Charles. Since then, I had been feeling that my days were numbered. I had always assumed that when the time came, I would be replaced by another quilt, but I guess Olinda didn't want to take the time to make a new one, or just chose not to.

Right before Christmas of 1948, Olinda had received her new winter edition of the Sears, Roebuck mail order catalog. In it, she found something called a chenille bedspread that she fell in love with. She told Lawrence it would be easier to launder, and it would look much nicer than the old worn quilt. She had gotten money from Anna and Edward as a Christmas present, and that was what she chose to spend it on.

I came to accept the news, as I had had my day, so to speak. I had truly enjoyed my time here but, to tell the truth, I was getting tired. All the pulling and twisting when they slept, and all the washings and hanging on the line had me feeling worn out. I felt like it was time for my retirement. I had decided that I wouldn't mind not being used, but I hoped I would still be able to observe what went on in the home. I wondered, too, where I would end up. I hoped I would still be able to see their faces every day! In any case, I was fully prepared the day my replacement came in the mail.

When Olinda came into the bedroom to put it on the bed, she pulled me off and laid me on the chair near the window. I was grateful for that so I could see what new bed covering she had chosen. She opened the package and revealed a bright blue spread. I had to admit … it was beautiful. There were flowers adorning the top of it, and the cloth draped all the way to the floor and around the sides of the bed from what I could see.

She adjusted and arranged till she had it just so, and it did look quite nice. It was not smooth like I was, but instead it had tiny raised lines with swirls and bumps. I didn't think it looked very comfortable, but with the sheet under it, I guessed it wouldn't be too bad. I figured the real test would be whether it kept them warm or not, because it didn't look very heavy. Of course, neither was I anymore.

Before I was relegated to wherever Olinda planned to put me, she was going to launder me one more time. I was truly dreading this day, and let me tell you why. She had not washed me for some time now, but I knew that when she did, it would be really uncomfortable.

One day last fall, I had heard Olinda and Lawrence talking about the new washing machine she had gotten. Before, she had always put me in a big tub of water and shoved me around on a board of sorts. Then she would wring me and put me in water again, and wring and squeeze me once more, and then she would hang me on the clothesline.

Now I was going to experience this new fandangled washing machine that, from what she described, had its own wringer on it. As she put me in the tub and added the soap, it didn't seem so bad. She turned the machine on and then shut the lid. That was when it got scary! I couldn't see anything, and it felt as if it would go on forever! I swished and swirled back and forth, jostled all around in that contraption!

By the time she came to get me, I was dizzy from the experience. But wait! The worst was yet to come! She then proceeded to run me through this fancy wringer and, wouldn't you know, it was ever so much worse than anything she had ever done to me! I felt like any life or hearing or vision I had before I went in there was surely going to be wrung out of me!

Once all the water was squeezed out, she finally hung me out on the clothesline. I felt like I had been beaten and left for dead. Luckily, there was just a mild breeze that day, and it lifted and bounced me in the air very gently. I don't think I could have handled a windy day. I vowed then and there to never complain about being put away, because I never wanted to go through that experience again!

When the time came to take me off the clothesline, Olinda folded me carefully and placed me back on the chair in the bedroom. That surprised me, because Lawrence sat on this chair nearly every day to put on his boots in the morning, and again at night to take them off. I had a feeling this would only be temporary, but she didn't return right away to remove me.

From this spot, I could look closer at the new bedspread. It really was quite nice, and I could see why she had chosen it. It brightened up the whole room, much more so than I had for a very long time. I was actually quite happy for them, for it had been a long time since Olinda had bought anything new for herself. As frugal as she was though, I was still surprised that she hadn't made another quilt. I guess with all the hours she spent sewing for others, making something for herself was a luxury that would just add more work to her day. In any case, this new bedspread would serve its purpose.

Later that day, Anna and Edward came to the house. I heard her say that they had brought Evangeline's old trunk with them. Anna said that she had no use for it anymore and asked if Olinda would like to have it for storage. She said she remembered how Olinda had said she wanted a cedar chest, so maybe Olinda could use this for storage until she got one.

Olinda thanked her mother and then helped her father rearrange furniture so the trunk could be placed in a corner of the parlor. Anna said that it seemed right to have the trunk back in Evangeline's home once again. She told Olinda that there were still a few things inside it—some fabric and old sheets— and maybe Olinda could use those for patching or for sewing projects, but that even with that, there was still a little bit of room inside.

The two women then came into the bedroom. I was so happy and surprised to see Anna! It was a rare treat to be in her presence again. I realized that this might be my last chance to look at Anna before Olinda put me away, and I gazed at her longingly. Since spending time in Lawrence and Olinda's home, I had missed all the contact with Anna and the mindful connection we had once had. Although my ability to see came after I was no longer in her home, I had had a few opportunities to see her and had memorized her appearance. I tried to make out her thoughts, as I had been able to do so very long ago, but there was no real spark there anymore.

I was saddened by that fact. I hadn't really looked at her closely for quite some time, and I noticed how much older she looked. She seemed shorter and more stooped, and she moved a little more slowly now. There were fine lines around her face, and her hair was turning a silvery white. I guess that is what happens when people grow old—they shrink and fade, just like I had.

Anna admired the new bed cover, and the two of them talked about Olinda's latest sewing project. She had been asked to make new window curtains for some of the rooms at the hospital in Robertsville. Olinda told Anna that pretty soon the old sewing machine might have to be replaced, because she had nearly worn it out. She had used it so much over the years. That, she said, was something she would be saving for, but she hoped this old one would hold out a bit longer.

Anna took a look at me sitting on the chair and mentioned that this old quilt had done its duty, and at least now there was somewhere for me to be placed. I wondered about that remark and tried to understand just what Anna meant.

As the two women left the room, I couldn't help but feel a little melancholy. So much had changed in my time with this family, and for it all to end now had me feeling sad and sorry for myself. I thought I had accepted my circumstances, but now I wasn't so sure.

As the day went on, I looked around this room

where I had spent so much time. I committed these images deep in my memory so I could reflect on them later on. I saw the photographs of family members lined up on the dresser, the ticking alarm clock, and the calendar, which—although it changed with each month and year—stayed in the same place on the wall above Olinda's sewing machine.

The crucifix hanging above the bed was my favorite; it was ornate and made of wood much like the bed's headboard and footboard, the smoothness of which I had become very familiar with. The chifforobe door was slightly ajar, and I could see clothing hanging inside and garments drooping out of a drawer that was not quite closed. I viewed these things with great sadness, because I would not be seeing this room much longer. I would not be able to watch as Olinda and Lawrence prepared for bed each night or readied for the day each morning. I would not feel their bodies resting under me as they slept on the bed. I had experienced so much in this room, and, oh, how I was going to miss it! It was almost more than I could bear.

After her parents had gone, Olinda came into the bedroom and picked me up. I studied her as she carried me. I had known Olinda since she was a little girl, watched her grow up and become a woman. I wanted to see her grow old like Anna as well.

I waited with anticipation to see where my new

home would be, and I was so very disappointed when she walked over to Evangeline's old trunk, lifted the top, and placed me in it. I had not expected this! Is this the reason Anna and Edward had brought the trunk today? Was this what she had referred to as the spot where I could be placed? I had been inside this trunk before, when I had been carried from Anna and Edward's home in town to the farm many years ago. Now, it seems, I was destined to live out my days inside it.

I had one last look at Olinda, and then she closed the lid on me. She had to keep rearranging my form to keep the lid closed. Obviously, the other things Anna had stored in the trunk took up more space than she had realized. It was much fuller than when I had previously occupied it, and fuller than Olinda had expected, too. She finally gave up and left the lid unlatched so that the heavy top was raised slightly.

As it turned out, this was my salvation! I could still see out through the small slit on three sides. I was overjoyed! If this is where I was to live out my days, however long that might be, I was in just the right place, for I could still see and hear all that was happening in the house. From this vantage point, I could actually experience even more than I had before!

If Olinda kept the trunk where it was now, I could see this room—the parlor—and also down the hall toward the bedroom, into the dining room, and even into the kitchen beyond. These were rooms I had only viewed when she took me through them to launder or patch me. I couldn't have asked for a better place!

That evening, when Lawrence came home, she showed him the new bedspread, and he said it looked fine to him, but what did he care as long as it kept him warm at night. He asked what she had done with me, and she showed him the trunk that her parents had brought that day. She asked him if he would look at the latch, because it would not shut properly.

He came over and opened the lid, jiggled the latch a few times, and tried again. He could not get it to close either; he told her that there was too much shoved inside it, and she would have to take something out so it would completely close. She sighed and said she would work on it tomorrow, but now it was time to make supper. Well, that got me a reprieve for the time being, I thought. Maybe she would forget about it tomorrow. I could only hope.

After supper, they sat down in the parlor and, as was their usual routine, Lawrence read the paper and Olinda took out her handiwork. I had always known that this was what they did in the evenings, and that they had the radio on in the background, but I had never seen them because the bedroom was too far away to see exactly what they were doing. As Olinda worked, she seemed to be using some sort of needle with a hook on one end, and she had a ball of yarn attached to it. She wound the yarn around her finger and made poking and pulling motions with the needle. She kept at this for a while, until the telephone rang and she got up to answer it.

James was apparently on the other end, and I heard her ask how he was doing. He and Patricia had both left for college in the fall the year before, after he had graduated high school. Things must have been going well for them in their first year. They were staying in separate rooming houses, but they were still fairly close to one another.

Olinda was telling James about the changes in the newspaper since he had been gone. She said that he would have to see it the next time he was home, that the layout was all different and Lawrence didn't care for it. She told James that he had better hurry up and finish school so he could come home and fix it. She laughed at something he said, and when she hung up, she told Lawrence that James had said he would get right on that situation when he came home in the summer—not that he could make any difference in the editor's decisions.

Olinda and Lawrence talked about the fact that James hoped to work for the newspaper again when he came home next month for the summer. She reported that James had said that Mr. Carner told him he had a job whenever he was available again. Lawrence said that he hoped Mr. Carner would keep his word, because it was good experience for James. With the classes he was taking at school, James was learning new things that might be beneficial to the town newspaper.

Just then, the telephone rang again, and Olinda got up to answer it. This time it was Gracie. I wondered if it was Thursday or if this was a surprise call. When Olinda was done talking on the hall telephone, she told Lawrence that Gracie and Charles were planning a visit tomorrow. It had been nearly a month since Lawrence and Olinda had seen them, and they agreed that it would be a very welcome visit.

Olinda smiled as she began her yarn work again and, after a time, she told Lawrence that maybe she would be crocheting baby booties soon. So that is what they called what she was doing—crocheting. It seemed like a fancy word for what she was creating with the needle and yarn, but I liked it. It was beginning to look like a blanket in several shades of blue. Years ago, I had heard Anna mention crocheting an afghan for baby Ollie. Now I was seeing the process firsthand.

Lawrence chuckled and told her it would be nice to have a grandchild, but maybe they were just coming to visit for no reason other than to see them. She went on to say that Gracie had let it slip that they were trying to conceive, so she knew it was on their minds.

The next day, when Gracie and Charles arrived, they took their jackets off and went into the bedroom to lay them on the bed, along with Gracie's purse. I heard them talking about the new bedspread, and Gracie exclaimed just how pretty it was. She then asked what her mother had done with "old faithful." She and Olinda laughed, and I had to wonder if she meant me, but I assumed she did. Olinda said that she had put the old quilt in the trunk and that, by the way, she had forgotten she couldn't close the lid properly.

She explained the problem and told them how Lawrence had said that it was just too full. Then Charles said he had an idea, and he proceeded to sit on the trunk while pushing the latch until it finally closed tight. Oh my, I was so disappointed! I could still hear, but now it was like years ago, when I could not see. I hadn't even gotten to see Gracie's beautiful face again before he had done it!

They all sat there talking until finally the young couple said they wanted to share some news. Gracie and Charles were indeed going to have a baby! How wonderful! Oh, how I wished I could have seen Olinda's face when Gracie and Charles told them. I bet she gave a knowing look toward Lawrence when they said it, and I missed seeing that!

Still, I realized that I was lucky to experience any of this, for if I had still been on the bed, I might not have heard any of it until Olinda and Lawrence had their evening talk. I missed those so much, but the late night conversations had been replaced with so many other daily interactions that I didn't give it much thought anymore. I felt I had had the best of both worlds, until Charles sat on the trunk and locked up my sight for good.

Shortly after the announcement, they all decided to go out to the farm to share the news with Anna and Edward. The house was quiet again, and I started thinking about how great it would be to have another baby toddling around this old house. Just then, there was a soft clicking sound and, just like that, the lid of the trunk popped back open. This time I had even more of a view than before. I waited to see who had created this opportunity for me, but no one was there. I could only think that maybe the latch was so old that it only caught because Charles had sat on it, and after a while it had released on its own. In any case, it worked to my advantage, because I could clearly see out into the room again. Indeed, I was quite content!

21

Olinda did not notice that the trunk was again not closed properly, and for the next year or so I was able to continue seeing all that went on in the house. Between my sight and my unfailing hearing, I kept up with nearly everything that took place there.

Although Olinda was a good housekeeper, routinely dusting and sweeping the rooms, it was apparent that either she couldn't see that the trunk was not fully shut or, if she could, she had decided that she didn't care, because nothing was done to fix it. She never did rummage through it for scraps like Anna had suggested, and that meant that I was left alone as well. I didn't care, because as long as I was right on top of the heap and could see out, I was happy.

Lawrence had a doctor's appointment right after the Christmas holiday, and he learned that his disease was still in remission. This was something the couple had been hoping for. Maybe he would be able to stop taking some of the medication he had been on since he learned of his illness, because it had been quite an expense for them all these years. The doctor agreed to decrease it, but still did not want to take him off it completely. The couple took this as a good sign though, and they hoped that the new year would bring better health for him and a healthy grandbaby as well.

Shortly after New Year's, Gracie gave birth to a little girl. They named her Marcia Anne. Olinda and Lawrence traveled to St. Louis to meet their first grandchild and were gone for a few days. They couldn't stop talking about the sweet baby after they returned home.

About a month later, the day came for Marcia Anne to be baptized at St. Joseph's. Gracie said that she had never really connected with the church in St. Louis and she felt more at home here in Parrie, so she wanted Marcia Anne to be baptized here. This was the first time I got to see the newborn. She was so tiny, and she had a full head of dark hair.

By this time, Gracie had finished nursing school and was working at the same hospital where Charles was completing his residency. She was on leave now, since she had just delivered Marcia, and she planned to take off work for several months.

After the ceremony, when everyone was gathered at the house for lunch, Olinda asked her what she would do with the baby when she went back to work. Gracie said she wasn't sure of their plans yet, but she still had some time to think about it. Charles still had a few more months of his residency, and then he would be able to either start his own practice or join a practice with another physician. No definite decision had been made on that front either. As Gracie said this, I saw her wink at Olinda. Olinda gave her a puzzled look, but the moment passed unnoticed by others.

James and Patricia arrived home from college the morning of the christening, and they were excited to meet James' new niece. They took turns holding her, as did Anna and Edward. Charles' parents, Jack and Millie, had also come to spend the day and help celebrate. They had driven from Chicago to St. Louis the day before and then traveled down to Parrie with Gracie and Charles and the baby.

As the family all sat down to dinner in the dining room, they left the sleeping baby in Gracie and James' old cradle in the parlor, right in front of me. I had plenty of time to study the infant and memorize that sweet little face. She really did look like an angel. It had been quite a while since I had seen James when he was that small, and I was fascinated.

The baby woke up and peered around, and for a moment it seemed that she was staring right at me. That gave me a strange sensation. No one else had paid any attention to me, since I could not easily be seen through the cracked opening of the trunk. Yet the more Marcia looked at me, the more deeply I felt her presence.

After the meal, Gracie came into the room to check on the baby and noticed that she was awake. She exclaimed how odd it was that Marcia hadn't cried when she awoke, but instead seemed content to look around at her surroundings. Charles had followed Gracie into the room, and he laughed and reminded her that Marcia couldn't see well yet—only shapes—and that she couldn't recognize faces or objects. Gracie agreed but she said Marcia was still a good baby for not crying while they ate their meal. Charles suggested that maybe she just wanted to be a good girl on her baptism day. That must be it, Gracie had replied.

Still, I had my reservations about this, because several times during the visit, when others were passing the baby around, it looked like she was turning her bobbing head toward me. I was amazed at how much she seemed to be drawn to me.

Later that day, when everyone had gone home and Lawrence and Olinda were sitting in the parlor, Olinda said that Gracie had whispered to her when she left that there was a possibility that Charles would open his practice right here in town. She said that with all the new growth because of the stove factory that had opened last year, people were moving in, and there was need for another doctor. The proximity to Robertsville Hospital was another positive factor for him.

Olinda said that it would be wonderful if that happened and that maybe Gracie could get a job at the hospital as well. Lawrence was doubtful about that, because he thought Gracie might not want to go back to work after Marcia was born. Olinda told him that he had a point, but that she would still pray for them to make their home in Parrie.

As in other times of worry or stress, Olinda got out her rosary, murmuring as she fingered each of the beads. I saw her do this more often now that I was in the parlor. In the bedroom, I had seen this rarely, although the couple had always knelt by the bed at night to say a few prayers. Other than when she was sewing or sleeping, Olinda didn't spend much time in the bedroom.

Since I had been in the parlor, I had often seen her take advantage of the quiet before bedtime for this ritual. It seemed that praying over her rosary had been a constant for her, just like it was for Anna before her.

The power of her prayers must have been strong, for within a few months, I heard Olinda tell Anna over the telephone that she had something to share. Gracie and Charles would be moving to Parrie very soon! Olinda was ecstatic conveying this news! Gracie had asked Olinda and Lawrence to keep an eye out for homes or land available. With so many people moving in, there wasn't much housing available.

Lawrence talked to Albert about an empty lot that was just a few blocks away. The owner of the lot was a friend of Albert's and agreed to sell it. While their new house was being built, Gracie and Charles were going to live with Lawrence and Olinda, taking over Gracie's old bedroom. James' bedroom would be used for Marcia's nursery. Olinda was so overjoyed about having family in her home again that she could hardly contain her excitement! She couldn't have been happier, and if she was happy, so was I.

Within just a few weeks, Charles, Gracie, and Marcia had moved into the once empty rooms of the house. There wasn't a spare inch of space now, with all the belongings they brought with them. Some of their extra furniture was stored out at the farm with Anna and Edward, and the rest was squeezed into every available spot in Olinda and Lawrence's home.

I was moved to a different corner of the parlor to make space for a rocking chair that Gracie used to rock Marcia to sleep. I didn't mind, because I still had a pretty good view of everything and, fortunately, no one seemed to know or care that the lid of the trunk was still unclasped.

As the young family settled in, everyone found their own routine. Gracie said that she didn't expect Olinda to do all the housework and cooking, that she wanted to do her part. Olinda balked at first, saying that it wasn't necessary and that she could continue to make their meals and she would definitely clean her own house. But Gracie insisted, telling Olinda that, after all, she and Lawrence were letting them disrupt their lives by living there. Olinda said that of course it was no imposition, and that she was over-joyed that they were there.

They worked out a schedule where Gracie would cook two nights a week and she would take turns with the laundry, too. After a while, Olinda came to enjoy her evenings off making supper, and she spent her time either crocheting or playing with Marcia.

By this time, Charles had joined the staff at the hospital in Robertsville and had set up his office in an empty storefront in Parrie. Gracie had decided not to go back to working in a hospital setting so that she could help him with his practice. Because it would take him some time to become fully established, she didn't join him at the office every day, and this gave her more time to spend with Marcia, too. Charles had hired an older woman, Evelyn, to be his secretary, and she and Gracie helped him set up the office fur-niture and equipment. This whole arrangement made Olinda very happy, because she got to babysit for Marcia when Gracie was working.

Marcia was now about five months old. She was rolling over, and sometimes when she was on her tummy, she would rock back and forth on her hands and knees. Olinda said it wouldn't be long before this little gal would be crawling. Gracie said she wasn't ready for her baby to be mobile, but Olinda told her that no amount of wishing your baby to stop growing would make it happen any differently. It was only a matter of time before Marcia would be into everything, she chuckled.

About this time, James returned home for the summer to work at the newspaper. Olinda had apparently spoken to him about offering Gracie and Charles his old room, and he had no problem with it whatsoever. He said that he would only be home a few months and then would be back at school again. Since there was no room for him to sleep in at Lawrence and Olinda's house, Patricia's parents had offered him the small carriage house at the back of their property, and they said he could stay there for the summer.

James stopped in one day when Olinda was home alone with the baby. He held out his hands to hold Marcia, and as he took her from Olinda, he mentioned that she had gotten so big since he had last seen her. He walked around the room, carrying her as he went. Olinda left the room for a few minutes, saying that she needed to do something and would be right back. As James walked around, Marcia started squirming in his arms; he called out to Olinda, saying that she was getting hard to hold onto and that he wanted to put her down.

Olinda came back in just then with her hands full, because she had just taken the linens off the baby bed to wash them. She said she would get a blanket so he could lay Marcia on the floor and Marcia could stretch out there—something she loved to do. Olinda told him to just hold her a minute more, until she could get back with a blanket.

After Olinda had left the room, James took matters into his own hands: He reached into the trunk and grabbed me out. He proceeded to place me on the floor and laid little Marcia on her back on top of me. She blinked at him and smiled, and he got right down next to her and shook a baby rattle in the air for her to grasp. I was happy as a lark to be used in such a way!

Olinda came back into the room with a clean blanket. She scolded James once she saw that he had used me to lay the baby on. He told Olinda that the baby was fine and that the old quilt would serve its purpose by keeping her off the bare floor. Olinda agreed that even though the quilt had been put away for a good year, she guessed it was still clean from its last laundering, so it was probably alright.

Just then, Marcia rolled over. She bent her head down close to me as if smelling me or trying to kiss me. I had such a feeling of contentment come over me. I remembered James himself lying on me as a baby, when Olinda sometimes changed his diaper on their bed. Now to have both of them stretched out on me was such an overwhelming feeling!

Marcia truly was a beautiful baby. The only other infant I had ever seen was James, for I gained my sight on the day of his baptism, but I didn't have any other basis for comparison. She continued to gaze at me intently, much as I in turn studied her features. Marcia had the most beautiful green eyes, somewhat like Anna's and Gracie's. Her middle name, Anne, had been chosen in honor of her great-grandmother. It seemed fitting that she should have the same shade of green eyes.

James continued to lie on the quilt with Marcia. She rocked back and forth and rolled over several more times, and after she did, he would reposition her on the quilt. He and Olinda caught up on family news while Marcia continued to play with the toy rattle.

Eventually, Marcia was facing me again and up on her knees. She sniffed me again, buried her face in me, and babbled. The vibration of her little voice against me was almost overpowering. She popped her head up again and looked right at me—and smiled the hugest smile I had ever seen. It literally lit up her whole face!

James must have seen this, because he told Olinda that little Marcie must really like this quilt, and he thought Olinda should use it all the time for her.

When Olinda objected to him calling the baby Marcie, he asked why on earth he shouldn't. Olinda just said that it was not their place to give the child a nickname unless her parents said it was okay. She didn't want to pin a name on the baby if they wanted her to be called the name that they had chosen.

He chuckled and told her that she was being silly, and if Gracie and Charles wanted to be mad at anyone, they could be mad at him. He thought the name Marcia sounded too old for this little one and that Marcie was perfect for her. He proceeded to plant a kiss on the baby's cheek, and she cooed back at him. He repeated the name Marcie several times, and each time he said it, she gave a soft belly laugh. Olinda smiled affectionately and told him that at least the baby wouldn't tell on him, since she couldn't talk yet.

22

That summer, Gracie went to work with Charles several days a week at the doctor's office. Olinda was in heaven to be spending so much time with Marcie. Apparently, the name had stuck. James had let it slip one day when he was home, and he called her Marcie in front of Gracie and Charles. Gracie was thrilled— she told James that she loved that version of the name! And everyone referred to her as Marcie from that day on.

Fairly often after that, I was placed on the floor to serve as a play space for Marcie, and my home was now on top of the trunk rather than in it, much to my delight. Every time Marcie was near me, she would put her face very close to me and study my fabric. One day, while Marcie was playing, she even fell asleep on me. Olinda left her there rather than move her to the crib, so as not to disturb her sleep. I was in love all over again.

Shortly after Gracie returned to work, Wallace and Felicity's son Harry volunteered for the war effort in Korea. He was sent directly into combat after basic training. Felicity was beside herself, knowing that he was playing such a role, but everyone said that he and others from town were heroes for joining up, and they felt that everyone should be very proud of the young men's patriotism. Needless to say, this gave Felicity little solace and she worried about him daily. Felicity, Anna, and Olinda started a prayer chain, praying for the end of yet another war. This new war affected the family much like when Anna's brother William had fought in World War I. Anna said that they had been lucky that none of their boys had had to fight in World War II, but now this new conflict was on their minds. Harry wrote home as often as he could, and he told them he felt like the United States had a very good chance of overcoming the enemy in that divided country.

By this time, Marcie had begun crawling, and Olinda had her work cut out for her keeping track of the baby's whereabouts. When Lawrence came home for lunch, sometimes he would play with her a little longer so Olinda could hang clothes on the line or sweep up the crumbs from the floor. She didn't want Marcie to be out of sight any longer than necessary.

When Gracie was home, she gave Marcie a little more leeway, and she told Olinda that she should do the same. Olinda replied that she had never felt this way about her own children. Back then, she would go about her day and let them play, but for some reason she felt like she needed to watch Marcie's every move.

Toward the end of the summer, Marcie had started pulling herself up to furniture, and Gracie happened to be home the day she took her first step. She yelled out to Olinda to come see, but by the time Olinda got there, Marcie had plopped down onto the floor again. Gracie picked her up and held her close, kissing the top of her head and saying she had gotten the best gift today. Even if she couldn't be home with her all the time, at least she got to witness this milestone.

Marcie was going to be an early walker, Olinda said, just like her mother was. Gracie asked how old she had been when she started walking, and Olinda told her that she had been about nine months old. Gracie replied that Marcie would be that age in another week, and it seemed that she was literally following in her mother's footsteps.

Fall seemed to come quickly that year, and soon it was nearing Christmas. In a few weeks, Marcie would be a one-year-old. By now, she was toddling around the house day and night. One night at supper, she was in her high chair and kept throwing her food on the floor. Undoubtedly, she was either not hungry or did not care for whatever Gracie had made that night. Every time Marcie threw her food on the floor, she would laugh and clap her hands and smile at everyone. One time, she even looked over toward where I sat on the trunk and appeared to wink at me. Oh my, I thought, she is a bundle of mischief!

Charles lightly rapped her hand the next time she did it and told her no, and she let out a loud wail. Her daddy had just broken her heart and ended her game! She buried her face in her hands and cried and cried. Finally, Gracie could take it no longer, and she picked her up out of the high chair and brought her into the parlor, laid me on the floor, and gave Marcie some toys to play with. She swung her arms and knocked all the toys over, and Gracie was at a loss as to what to do. She scolded Marcie over this tantrum and told her that she needed to behave.

Just like that, Marcie grabbed a corner of me and pulled as much of me as she could into her arms, rested her head on me, and stuck her thumb in her mouth. Gracie exclaimed that this was new—apparently Marcie had found a security blanket! I wondered what that meant, but I was happy to be feeling Marcie squeezing me contentedly as she settled down.

After that, Marcie wouldn't let me alone. She would drag me into her bedroom at night, but apparently I was a little large to be placed in the crib with her as she wanted. They tried giving Marcie other smaller blankets to snuggle with, but she would not have them and tossed them aside.

Eventually, Olinda had a solution. Since I was no longer being used on the bed and was so very threadbare, she cut off a section of me from near the bottom, which was not as worn as my middle had become.

I wondered how this was going to affect me, but it was such a small square—only one of my fan-shaped blocks—that I didn't feel any different. Olinda sewed the raveled edges several times with her sewing machine, and where she had cut me, she repaired the larger part of me as well. Now there were two of me! I wondered if I could be in two places at once, and didn't have to wait long to find out.

Wherever Marcie went, I went with her. The part of me that was mostly whole went back into the trunk and was just an extension of me, I assumed. I never had the sensation of being inside the trunk at that time. It was as if my heart and soul, my entire being, was inside the tiny quilt that Marcie claimed as her own. I had never been so content. Any other feelings I had up to now paled in comparison. This was my icing on the cake of life, I thought.

Everywhere Marcie went, she dragged me with her. I went to bed with her every time she slept—her little thumb in her mouth and me squished under her arm. She clutched me in her chubby little hand morning, noon, and night. I went to church with her for the first time ever for Christmas Eve mass, and that was an experience in itself. All the beautiful singing and the twinkling lights, I truly thought there was no greater joy. It was such a moving experience and one I wouldn't soon forget.

The next morning, Marcie received several new

toys and some clothes. As she played with her new doll, she wrapped me around it and held me tight. I felt that I was truly living, in a way I had never experienced before. At this point, I felt more loved and cherished than I ever had, and it made me so proud to be a comfort to her in a way I had never been for Lawrence and Olinda. I had found another purpose here, I realized.

Shortly after New Year's Day in 1951, Marcie celebrated her first birthday. I was right there in her arms as she devoured her birthday cake. By the time she was through, I looked like I had been dragged through a mud puddle, with chocolate icing smeared all over me. That set up quite an ordeal, because Gracie and Olinda had a hard time getting me away from Marcie to launder me. Somehow they must have distracted her and gotten the job done though, because by bedtime I was as good as new, and Marcie was clinging to me with her chubby little hands again.

I still found it odd that I had no sensation of being in two places at once, and I could not quite figure out why all my feelings, hearing, and sight were concentrated in my one square of fabric. I had no sense of direction or measurement, but if I had to guess, I would say that my size was now about the size of one of Olinda's pillows on the parlor sofa. In any case, I was just the perfect size for Marcie to hold onto.

One day, we were in the parlor, and I noticed the

trunk and saw that it was still unlatched but that the lid seemed to be evenly closed. Maybe this was why I was not able to see two things at once—the rest of me was in a completely dark place. Needless to say, I was very grateful that even though I was only a fraction of my former self sizewise, all my experiences and memories were with the part of me that was spending time with Marcie.

That spring, I overheard daily updates on the house that Gracie and Charles were building. They had waited to break ground until the winter thaw, and now things must have been progressing smoothly, because I heard Gracie tell Olinda that they hoped to have it completed and be moved in by the end of summer.

Olinda said she wasn't looking forward to that day, because that would mean the family would not be living with them anymore. Gracie laughed and reminded Olinda that they were only moving two blocks away, and she would still see Marcie on the days Gracie worked at the office, so she shouldn't despair. While the house was taking shape, the whole family went over to see the progress one day, me in tow, of course, tucked safely under Marcie's arm.

I couldn't imagine what it would look like when it was finished, but from what I could tell, there was still a lot to be done, because there were no walls yet, just sticks holding up the top of it. The top of the house was called the roof, Charles explained to Marcie, as he pointed out the rafters overhead. Some birds had nested in the eaves over the long rainy weekend, and Charles got up on a ladder that had been left by the workmen and moved the nest to a tree in the yard. He said he hoped the birds could make their home somewhere else instead of inside theirs.

Before he moved it, he showed the nest with two blue eggs in it to Marcie, explaining that there were baby birds inside. Marcie just looked at them intently. Her vocabulary was still very limited; she only said a few words like "mama" and "dada" and "bye-bye," but that day she said the word "bird"—only it sounded like "bur" and they all laughed at her attempt. Gracie said Marcie was learning so much every day, and by the time they moved into the house, she would no doubt be talking even more.

A few days later, while Marcie was playing, she dropped me on the floor and didn't realize it. I noticed it right away, but I could do nothing about the situation. Marcie had been sitting on the floor behind one of the chairs in the parlor, and that is where I lay, unbeknownst to anyone else. Eventually, Marcie must have missed my warmth and comfort, because she started calling out to her mama.

Gracie was home from the office for lunch that day, and she picked Marcie up and sat her in the highchair to eat. Marcie wouldn't take one bite, and she just kept saying something that Olinda and Gracie couldn't understand.

Finally, Olinda asked Gracie where I was, and they realized that that was what she was trying to tell them. They looked high and low; finally, after much searching, they found me behind the chair. The grownups in the household had been referring to me as her blankie, and they finally realized that she had been saying her own version of the word. From that day on, I was known as Marcie's "Kiki."

At the end of the summer, Gracie and Charles were packing up to move into their new house. Olinda was having a hard time dealing with the fact that she would no longer have them with her, especially Marcie, and she remarked how quiet the house would be when they were gone. Gracie reminded her that they were welcome to visit as often as they liked, and that Marcie would still be coming to spend days with Olinda when Gracie worked.

As for me, I was overjoyed to be going somewhere new. Not that I didn't love all the time I had spent with Olinda and Lawrence, and my years at Anna and Edward's as well, but this was a whole new experience for me. I was never far from Marcie's side, and I loved all the attention.

Moving day turned out to be a very hot one, but the heat didn't seem to bother Marcie. She clung to me the same as always. The men made quick work of loading everything up onto trucks and wagons, with Lawrence and James helping Charles secure the items with ropes. By the time all their possessions were in place, along with some new appliances and furniture they had bought for the home, I was a sweaty, slobbery mess. It seemed that Marcie was cutting more teeth, and she always seemed to be drooling on me.

That day, when Gracie put Marcie in the crib for a nap, I was all gathered up under Marcie, so I couldn't see her new bedroom very well. Later, Gracie quietly tip-toed in and freed me. She quickly set me in a pan of water to soak with some laundry soap and then wrung me out after a while, hanging me up to dry in the bathroom. I wondered if Gracie had a clothesline like Olinda, or if maybe she just didn't take the time to hang me outside. In any case, I was hung above the bathtub, where the nearby open window was letting in a soft breeze that dried me quickly.

While I was hanging there, I looked around at my surroundings and thought how wonderful this new home was. It was far different and more modern than any of the other homes I had lived in.

Through the open window, I could see a neighboring house across the yard and a tree right near the window. Wouldn't you know, there was that bird's nest sitting on a far branch. I wondered if those eggs that Charles had shown Marcie had ever hatched, and if the baby birds were now grown and living there.

23

Living in Gracie and Charles' new home was a totally different experience for me. Charles kept odd working hours: He had appointments with patients at his office, and then he went to the hospital, which took up the better part of his day. When he came home in the evening, he would play with Marcie just like he did when the young family lived with Olinda and Lawrence.

Sometimes, as before, he would be called away. Gracie didn't seem to mind; I guessed she was used to this by now. She and Marcie would play or visit with friends or family, and a lot of nights they ate supper alone, but sometimes Charles was there too.

I loved the new bedroom for Marcie at this house. It was painted a pretty pink color, and it had a dresser with a lamp on it, as well as a closet, which was something I had never seen before. There were doors that opened into a space where all her clothes hung on hangers, and her shoes were kept in there as well. There was a bookshelf in the room for her books— some of Charles and Gracie's old ones and also new ones that Marcie had been given.

There was a wooden box on the floor, loaded with

dolls and other toys. I heard Gracie call it a toy box as she helped Marcie pick up all the things she had left lying around before she went to bed at night. Marcie was such an obedient little girl. As I observed how quickly she picked up mannerisms and language of the adults around her, I realized just how smart she was.

Something new that would eventually occupy a fair amount of the time I spent in this house was a television set. When they were all moved in, Charles said that he had a surprise for Gracie, but that it wasn't here yet. A week or so later, a truck arrived with a delivery. Charles happened to be home for lunch that day and helped the delivery man unload and set up the new contraption. He told Gracie to stay out of the living room until everything was ready.

Having a living room was new to me. Olinda and Anna had both called the room they spent relaxing time in their parlor. I guessed that people gave this space a new name in the newer homes, because Charles and Gracie referred to this room as the living room.

In any case, once the television was all set up, Gracie was allowed into the living room, with Marcie and me following behind. Gracie was overwhelmed and said it was something she had not expected. Charles told her he thought it would help pass the time when he was gone on calls and that Marcie would probably enjoy the children's shows during the day.

Marcie plopped down on the floor to watch while the two men showed Gracie how to turn it on. Before I knew it, I could hear people talking like on the radio, but I could see them, too! I was mesmerized, and so was Marcie, as we tried to keep up with the action on the screen. This was just like what Lawrence and Olinda had described after they saw a television a few years ago, but now I was getting to experience it for myself.

Oh my, it was a wonder! They turned a knob and adjusted the volume and fiddled with another one to adjust the picture screen. They showed Gracie how to change the channels with yet another knob. It all seemed confusing to me, but Gracie was fascinated. She had seen a television before but had never been able to choose her own shows and stations, they called them.

They flipped back and forth through different channels until they came to one showing a woman playing with puppets. Gracie said that Marcie should like this one. She had heard about *Kukla, Fran and Ollie* from her friend Shirley, who had mentioned that it was a favorite of her nephew's. Marcie was enthralled, having never seen anything like it, and she squeezed me tight as she sucked her thumb and watched the show.

I was intrigued as well, listening to the woman interacting with the puppets on the television set. I was amazed—it was almost as if these people were here in the room with everyone.

As time went on, the family would often gather in the living room to enjoy many of the shows on the new television. During the day, it was turned on so Gracie could watch shows, and also so Marcie could watch *Kukla, Fran and Ollie, Time for Beany,* or other children's shows. It was surely an interesting gadget to have in the new home, and one that I quickly fell in love with.

One day, Marcie left me lying on the floor for a while, and I got a glimpse of a man talking about the weather and how it was going to rain that day. Sure enough, the room darkened later, clouds blotted out the sun, and it thundered and rained, just like the man had said it would. I was suspicious that he knew this ahead of time and wondered just how he had predicted this.

On the days Gracie worked, I tagged along with Marcie to Olinda's house, of course. I was back in familiar territory there, for I had learned every nook and cranny of Olinda's home as Marcie wandered through it after claiming me for her own.

Olinda was overjoyed to have Marcie back on those days, and they played endlessly with blocks and dolls. Before Marcie's nap, Olinda read her story books. It fascinated me to watch her read these books to Marcie; that was something I had never experienced before. The scenes on the pages seemed to reach out to me, and I was interested in the tales that Olinda told as they turned the pages.

Marcie's favorite story was one called *The Gingerbread Man,* and she had apparently memorized some of the words as Olinda read them over and over again at her request. While she turned the pages, Marcie would sometimes point to the pictures and call out words that she remembered when she saw the illustrations. Olinda would exclaim "yes!" and hug her tight and kiss the top of the toddler's head. I was always included in these hugs, and they made me feel so wonderful!

That year at Christmas, Marcie was given a new puppy. I had never seen a dog like this one before. Olinda and Lawrence had had an old hunting dog, and I remembered hearing dogs barking outside at Anna and Edward's home at the farm as well, but the dogs were never allowed inside.

This one, it seemed, was meant to stay inside the house. It was such a tiny thing, and it looked like one of Marcie's toys. I would describe this animal as a panting ball of black fluff. I heard Charles tell Gracie that it was a Scottish terrier, and so the puppy was given the obvious name of Scottie. At night, he slept on a pallet near the stove in the kitchen, right next to a water and food dish that Gracie had for him.

Marcie was fascinated with the puppy, and she carried the pup—along with me—all around the house. I don't think they remembered to let him outside one time, because I was christened one day. Marcie kept yelling "my Kiki wet!" Of course, that meant another laundry day for me. My, my, he was a handful for Marcie, but she seemed to manage him, and the dog took to her right away.

Sometimes Scottie was too much for Marcie to hold onto, so he took to tagging along behind or beside her. He would often sit in her lap while she played on the floor or watched the television. The dog had such short legs that he reminded me of the stool that Lawrence used to prop his feet on when he sat in his chair in the parlor.

The pup seemed to bounce rather than walk, and his presence was always announced by the jingling of the little tag on his collar. He rarely barked, but when he did, it was quite unlike the howl of the old hunting dogs. He yipped and yapped when he needed to go outside or wanted attention. To me, he seemed like a nuisance, but the family seemed very happy with him, and he was a playmate for Marcie.

By the time Marcie turned two, Scottie had left his mark in many places in the house. The linoleum floors must have been easy to clean, because I never heard Gracie complain even a single time about the messes he left. After a while, he must have gotten trained properly, because those mishaps seldom happened anymore.

It was about this time that Gracie was also trying to train Marcie to use the bathroom. One day, when Olinda stopped by, she and Gracie were talking about how Marcie was dry all day but still had problems at night. Olinda told her that was a good first step. Hopefully, Marcie would start to understand it soon and wouldn't have to wear diapers at all anymore.

Before long, Marcie was following in Scottie's footsteps, because she began dragging me into the bathroom to her little chair. She was growing so much by this time that Charles told her that big girls need a big bed, and she moved from the baby bed to a child-sized bed—low to the ground so she could climb right in for her naps and at nighttime. Marcie was so proud of that new bed that whenever company came, she took them into her room to show it to them.

One night, as Gracie was reading bedtime stories to Marcie, Marcie complained of something yucky in her bed. Gracie told her that there was nothing there, but Marcie kept insisting. Finally, Gracie threw back the covers—and revealed a pile of cut-up leftover syrupy pancakes that she had fed to Scottie that morning.

At the time, Gracie felt that the dog had eaten them pretty quickly, and she had even exclaimed that he must have inhaled the food. Apparently, he wasn't eating them at all, but had hidden them in Marcie's unmade bed for safekeeping, perhaps planning to return for them later. Scottie, who was sitting by the bed, got a good scolding. Whether he understood or not, I don't know, but Gracie had to strip the bed and put fresh sheets on for Marcie and me to sleep in that night. After that, Gracie kept a closer eye on Scottie, or maybe he had learned his lesson, because no more food was found hidden in Marcie's bed.

A few months later, springtime was back again. Trees and flowers were blooming outside, and Gracie was back at Olinda and Lawrence's for the day. Lawrence came home at lunchtime to eat with them, and since it was such nice weather, Olinda decided to have a picnic out under an old oak tree in the backyard. To my surprise, she spread out the rest of me under the tree. I was so surprised to see this! I scrutinized my other half, or rather, most of me. That part of me hadn't changed a bit, but the portion of me used by Marcie was getting a little worse for wear—more faded and threadbare, like my middle.

Marcie noticed where a piece was missing, and she told Olinda that the quilt looked like her Kiki. Olinda explained how she had made Marcie's Kiki and showed her where the piece had been cut off. She then took me from the child's hand and laid it right in the spot where I had been cut off. Marcie looked at me for a while and then back to the rest of the quilt, over and over again. She finally looked at Olinda and told her that Grandma was a big girl, and she needed the big Kiki.

Olinda and Lawrence laughed at this. They told her that Grandma didn't need a Kiki, but that someday Marcie could have the whole thing. Olinda assured Marcie that she would sew me back on for her so that she could have the big Kiki. Marcie smiled and seemed satisfied with that answer, and then plopped down on me—her Kiki square—to eat her lunch, directing Lawrence and Olinda to the larger part. They both laughed at her bossiness and then did as they'd been told.

After they had finished eating and gone back inside, Felicity came running over from next door, saying they had just received word that Harry had been wounded. She didn't know all the details, just that his injuries were not life-threatening. She had spoken to Harry himself: He was being sent stateside to a hospital in Washington, D.C. and would return home after his recuperation. He had had time for only a hurried conversation with his mother, telling her that he had been injured and would get in touch with her when he was back in the States.

Felicity was fretting over what his injuries could

possibly be, but Olinda reassured her that it was a good sign that she had been able to speak with Harry himself rather than with another officer. That alone should be a great comfort to her. Lawrence also reassured her that since Harry was coming home, he would not likely be sent back anytime soon, if at all. Felicity said she hoped not, because her nerves couldn't handle it again.

Anna and Edward came by the house later. They had gone to Wallace and Felicity's once they had heard the news. They, too, felt that it was definitely a good sign that Harry had been able to talk to his mother, and hopefully his injuries would not be too debilitating. Later on, they found out that Harry had to have two fingers amputated from his left hand. They all felt that it could have been so much worse, and Felicity was thankful that he had not lost his whole hand. It would be another month or so before he returned home to Parrie.

PART THREE

24

When Harry came home from the service in October 1952, he seemed to adjust very well to the loss of the ring and pinkie fingers of his left hand. A small portion of the hand had also been amputated, but he adapted quickly. Luckily, he was right-handed, so he was able to function quite well. He recuperated at home for another month or so and then went back to work at the quarry.

Harry's previous job at the quarry was too strenuous for him now, since he no longer had enough strength in his left hand, so Felicity turned her office and driving duties over to him, saying that she was ready to retire from that position. She was sad that both her boys had debilities: Harry had lost part of his hand in the war, and Ollie had a limp from his sports injuries. Nevertheless, they were lucky that they were still strong young men and were able to compensate for their injuries in many ways.

Shortly after Marcie's third birthday, Gracie and Charles announced that they were expecting another baby. Marcie was so excited—she wanted the baby to come right now! Gracie assured her it that would be several months before the baby arrived. Marcie also kept insisting that she wanted a baby brother. Even though Gracie told her that it might be a sister, Marcie declared that the baby would be a boy.

By this time, Marcie was needing me less and less, and some mornings I found myself left in the bed, on the floor, or on a nearby chair. One day, Scottie dragged me out of the bed and hid me behind the toy box in Marcie's room. She didn't ask for me at all that day, and it was nearly bedtime when Gracie found me. I felt that my days as her security blanket were coming to an end. Gracie noticed this, too, and she sometimes reminded Marcie that she had left her Kiki lying around.

In July, Gracie gave birth to another girl, named Catherine Elizabeth. Marcie was not happy about this, and she kept insisting that they needed to send the baby back for a brother instead.

Olinda sat with Marcie one day and explained that she herself had always wanted a sister to play with, but that she had two older brothers who never wanted to include her in their activities. She told Marcie that now that she was a big sister, she could show Catherine all the things she had learned, and someday they would be best friends. After that, Marcie was often seen kissing the baby's tiny feet or patting her arm when she cried. She would tell Catherine that everything was okay and fuss over her like a mother hen with her chick. It was comical to see.

One day, when Catherine was particularly fussy, Marcie brought me to the baby while Gracie was holding her. She said that maybe her Kiki would keep the baby from crying. Gracie laid me over the baby's tummy, but even though Catherine quieted somewhat, she was still fidgety. Nevertheless, from that day on, I was left to Catherine, and Marcie never asked for me or needed me again. Sometimes Marcie would look at me fondly, as though she regretted her decision, but then she would remind everyone that she was a big sister now and didn't need me.

Sadly, as Catherine grew, she never needed a Kiki, so I was folded up and put away in a drawer. I was sad that my time with Marcie had been so short-lived, but I was not in a position to protest. I could still hear the sounds of the household, like when I was in the trunk, but I was never pulled out and used again.

About this time, there was another wedding in the family: James and Patricia were married at St. Joseph's. They had graduated from college and moved to St. Louis so they could both pursue jobs in their respective fields. James found work as an assistant editor for one of the top newspapers, and Patricia found a job teaching high school mathematics. When he was younger, James had wanted to work for the newspaper in Parrie, but when he spoke with the editor after he had gotten his degree, they could not come to terms on a salary that suited him.

Olinda and Lawrence were sad to see them go, but they understood that James and Patricia needed to make their own decisions about their lives. The young couple visited Parrie often, and after several years they added to their family with two sons, born a year apart. Olinda and Lawrence were very happy that James and Patricia frequently brought their boys back to Parrie to visit.

As Marcie and Catherine grew older, Gracie regularly sorted through their clothing and passed things along that the girls could no longer wear. One day, as part of her sorting, Gracie took me out of the drawer, placed me in a sack, and took me to Olinda's house. She suggested that maybe Olinda could put the quilt back together and save it for Marcie. Olinda did just that: She repaired my torn spots and sewed me back into my own little corner of the quilt. I had mixed feelings about all of this, but I was extremely grateful for the extra time I had spent with Marcie. I hoped that one day she would remember me, but since she was so young, I very much doubted that she would.

When Olinda finished patching me up, she did exactly what I suspected she would do. She folded me up and put me in the trunk. However, this time, the latch stuck fast, and I immediately lost all opportunity to see what was going on around me. This made me very, very sad. I knew my usefulness had come to an end, and I had a feeling that I would be stuck in this trunk for years to come. I was not looking forward to only being able to hear what was going on in the house and never seeing my family again.

25

Over the remainder of my years in Olinda's house, I overheard enough of the everyday conversations to keep me aware of how my family was doing. So many times I wished to be able to see the family as I once had, but alas, this was not meant to be.

Two events distressed me no end. I learned that Edward had died and the family was in mourning. I wondered how Anna was getting along without him. One day, I could pick out her voice among a lot of people talking. I tried and tried to make out what they were saying, and eventually I understood that Anna was coming to live with Olinda and Lawrence. I guessed she was lonely out at the farm by herself, and maybe she had health problems of her own. From what I gathered, the family had sold the farm because no one in the family wanted to live in the big old house or take care of the property.

A short while later, Lawrence's illness returned, and Olinda had her hands full taking care of him and helping Anna. Then just a few months after Edward had passed, so did Lawrence, and the family suffered yet another loss. Olinda and Anna were very quiet in the house after that, and I could only imagine them sitting in their chairs, rosary beads in hand.

I was very distressed that my family was enduring such sorrow. I thought back over all my years with the family, and I realized just how much I had experienced with them—the births, the deaths, the weddings, the moves to new homes. I had had a full life, and now I was tired and old, just like Anna. I felt that I might be destined to stay in Evangeline's trunk forever, forgotten in a corner of Olinda's parlor. If that was to be the case, I almost wished I could not hear anything going on, because that only left me wanting more. I had once felt so fulfilled and content, and now I was desolate beyond belief.

When Anna moved into the home, she brought a lifeline for me though. She brought a television set with her, and it came to be my constant companion. Olinda and Lawrence had never seen the need to purchase one, because they relied on the radio for their news and entertainment. Now, since the television sat right next to me, I could easily hear what was going on when Olinda and Anna watched their shows. They often left the television on even when they were not in the room—just for the noise, I guess. After the deaths of Edward and Lawrence, Anna and Olinda were both terribly sad and missed their husbands very much. Of course, I could not see the images on the screen, shut away in the darkness of the trunk as I was, but it kept me occupied to listen to it.

Anna and Olinda both enjoyed something they called soap operas. I had heard some of these on the radio over the years, but now they were broadcast on the television as well. Some days they watched several different soap operas, and I heard them talking about how much they looked forward to finding out what would happen in the characters' lives the next day. One day, they watched a news broadcast when a new president took office. He seemed to be well loved by them—he was a very handsome young man, and he was Catholic like their family. Anna and Olinda said this man would be so good for the people of this country.

When the house was quiet at night, I would reminisce about all that I had seen and done over the years. I reflected on the times I had spent in Anna's house; then when I lived with Olinda and Lawrence and was a comfort to them; the years when Gracie and James were living at home; and later still, my precious time with Marcie.

How the times had changed! The noises coming from the television, the news segments covering another war overseas in a faraway country called Vietnam ... and the music that was popular now! It was so different from what I had heard years ago on Anna's phonograph! Times were changing for everyone, and I had a feeling that things were going to be changing even more.

When Catherine was born, Gracie had decided to stay home with both girls. She had not gone back to work in Charles' doctor's office. I am sure this was another part of Olinda's sadness, because the girls were not around nearly as much. They would stop by to visit often, but they never stayed long enough to suit Olinda and Anna.

Eventually, when Catherine was big enough to join Marcie at school, Gracie returned to work. For several years now, the two girls had been coming to stay with Olinda and Anna every day after school until their mother got home from work. I liked those times best. Even though I could not see their faces, I could hear them if they were in the parlor. I would hear them playing cards with their grandmothers, asking for help with their homework, and enjoying popcorn and soda pop or homemade cookies and milk. I wished so much that I could see their faces once again.

It was a happy day for me when I overheard the good news that Gracie was expecting again. Olinda was overjoyed by this, because the girls were getting bigger and she said it would be nice to have another baby in the house soon. Hopefully, the baby would spend a lot of time with her and Anna, if Gracie went back to work after the baby was born. Some time later, I overheard someone say that Gracie was expecting twins. That seemed to run in the family, because Caroline and Albert had had twin sons 25 years ago.

One day, when the girls were there after school, Catherine asked Olinda what was in the box in the corner. Olinda explained it wasn't a box, but a trunk. My hearing perked up when I heard them speaking. Olinda told Catherine that Anna had gotten the trunk from a very dear old friend. Anna added that once she didn't have a need for it anymore, she had passed it on to Olinda to use.

Catherine asked if she could see what was in it, and Olinda told her she could. The young girl opened the lid, and a rush of fresh air came over me. It was quite a welcome relief from the stale mustiness! I gazed at Catherine, having not seen her since she was very small. She was such a lovely child! She took me out and exclaimed that she bet I used to be pretty.

Anna asked Catherine to bring me over to her. I could see that Anna was sitting in a different kind of chair, one with wheels—something I had never seen before. I didn't understand why she sat in this special chair until I saw Olinda roll it a little closer to the trunk. That's when I realized that maybe Anna could not walk or get around like she had before. I gazed into her face, and I saw just how very old she had become. It made me sad to think that I had not had a chance to see her as a young woman when she had made me but, nevertheless, I was so very happy to lay eyes on her for what I felt might be the last time.

Anna explained to Catherine that she had made me as a wedding gift for Olinda and Lawrence, and that she had made it many, many years ago, when Olinda herself was just a little girl. Catherine asked her great-grandmother just how long it had taken, and Anna answered with a short laugh, saying that it took longer than she would have liked, but that it was well worth it. She explained that she had made many quilts before and after this one, but that this one had been made with more love, since she had made it for her only daughter.

Olinda smiled at her mother. She said that she and Lawrence sure did make use of the quilt until she had finally retired it years ago for that old chenille bedspread—and did Anna remember that? They both laughed about how the bedspread hadn't held up nearly as long as the quilt. The old bedspread was long gone now, and here was this lovely old quilt, still held together, even if not by much.

Olinda told Catherine that the quilt that had recently been placed on her bed would probably be the last one she made. Olinda said her hands were getting too arthritic to quilt anymore, and Anna's eyesight was failing too much to help her. She said it was a good thing she had made wedding quilts for Catherine and Marcie when she was a little younger.

Just then, Marcie came into the room. She had apparently been in the kitchen doing homework when her sister took me out of the trunk. My, how she had grown! Such a tall, pretty young lady she had become! Her arms were no longer short and chubby, but were now long and slender. I gazed into her face. She was no longer a baby at all, and she seemed to be growing into a beautiful young woman. She had changed so much!

Marcie exclaimed that she remembered this quilt. She pointed to the corner and asked Olinda, was this Kiki? She recognized me! Oh my, that made me so happy! Olinda assured her that it was, and that she had sewn me back together once Marcie didn't need a security blanket anymore. Olinda went on to say that someday, when Marcie wanted me, she could take me to her own house. She said I wasn't much good for anything anymore, but maybe Marcie would find a use for me. I really and truly hoped that that would happen someday. I now had hope that I wouldn't be stuck for eternity in the trunk.

Marcie said she knew that her great-grandmother had had names for all the quilts she made, and she wondered what this one was called. Anna said it was Grandmother's Fan, still one of the prettiest patterns to make. Olinda added that it had been so useful and beautiful in its prime. Then Anna remarked that the double wedding ring quilt that Olinda had made for Gracie and Charles was equally pretty. The two women spent some time reminiscing about all the quilts they had made over the years as they took several other items out of the trunk.

I was intent only on observing all of them so that I could hold their images deep within me. Olinda had also aged, but not nearly as much as my dear Anna. I looked from one to the other, and then at the young girls once again. If only Gracie were here to complete the circle of women I had come to know in my life! As they started putting things back in the trunk, Gracie walked into the house. I was so happy to see her! She was obviously pregnant, her tummy stretching the fabric of her blouse.

I felt very sad to know that if I was put away again, I would not get to see the new babies. I hoped I would get one more reprieve, but I knew this was not likely to happen. I felt that today was probably my only chance to see them all together again. To have all the women of this family in one room and be able to see their loving faces was all that I could have hoped for! I rejoiced in the fact that this dream had come true.

Gracie was such a beautiful woman and her lovely green eyes, so much like Anna's, gleamed as her daughters talked about all they had been hearing from the two older women. She rested her hands on her swollen abdomen as she listened to them. Gracie told the girls that they could learn a lot from their grandmothers, and she wished that they could have been taught to quilt, too. Anna and Olinda had taught her, she said, but she didn't know how to quilt very well. Still, she and Olinda would try to teach the girls someday, and the new babies, too, if they were girls. Seeing these sweet young girls, with their bright inquisitive faces, made me realize that I had come full circle.

Anna ran her hands over me once more before I was taken away. I saw her beautiful eyes one last time. They were not as clear as they had once been, but they were deeply embedded in my soul. Olinda put everything back in the trunk, and then she took me from Anna and put me right on top, patting me down a little. She sighed, and then she smiled fondly at me one last time while I gazed at her as she lowered the lid of the trunk.

How many times had I seen Olinda's warm, smiling face as she tended to me in one way or another? A true feeling of melancholy came over me as she closed the lid, the latch closing tight. Little did I know that this would be my very last time seeing her as well.

26

They say that life is short, but I felt that I had been with this family for so very, very long. I was ever so grateful for every moment, every day, every year. I had been able to spend time with them for much longer than I had ever anticipated, and I had received reprieves over and over again after serving my original purpose.

I had been given a tremendous gift, by a benefactor still unknown, but I cherished every memory I had ever made. Why I had been chosen to connect with these women and their families was still beyond my comprehension. I had grown to love each and every one of them, and I had felt so much a part of their lives. I thought about all the places I had been with them, their homes that I had been used in, and all the faces I had come to love.

Shortly after that momentous reunion, something happened to Anna. I heard snippets of conversation, too muffled to understand clearly, but I feared the worst for her. Life as I had come to know it drastically changed. I felt myself drifting, as if I were in some large body of water or floating through the air. I had the feeling that whatever befell Anna that fateful day had overtaken me as well.

After that, I never experienced sight or sound again: no sight because of the darkness inside the trunk, and not even an ability to hear what was going on in the home anymore. Meeting the soon-to-be-born twins was not meant for me to experience.

One day, I had the vague sensation of the trunk being lifted and carried. I sensed that I and the trunk were going somewhere, but I had no idea where. All I know is that a door closed a short time later, and that was the end of it.

EPILOGUE

People wandered around outside the old house, inspecting all the items placed on the lawn. There was a wagon loaded with boxes of dishes and kitchenware, another laden with old tools and garden implements, and still others that held more household items and knick-knacks. Furniture and appliances dotted the yard near the old garden. Over by the ancient weeping willow tree sat an old car and truck. These were the remnants of the life of a family—so many belongings accumulated by the now-deceased owner, who had passed away a few months earlier at the age of 98.

The auctioneer banged his gavel onto his wooden lectern and called out, "Sold to bidder number 107!", and the new owner of a metal step stool picked up his prized possession. The onlookers moved toward the vehicles, which were scheduled next on the auction block. It could be said that there was not a very large crowd here, but yet many people had turned out for the event. Some had come just for curiosity's sake rather than with an intent to purchase something. Others placed small piles of their treasures on the

ground or held them in boxes, adding to their pur-
chases now and then as the auction continued.

Near the shed where it had been stored sat an old
trunk. It had probably been lovely in its heyday, but
now, with some water damage and the leather peel-
ing and crumbling off the handles, it sat forlornly
among an old wicker basket, some straw brooms, and
a wooden ironing board. Next to it, a clothesline
stretched from one post to another. It held a number
of colorful old quilts and blankets, some more worn
than others. One in particular looked as though it had
been heavily used; it had been patched and sewn over
so many times—its once vibrant colors long since
faded, its owner recently gone, its maker having
passed 40 years ago.

Several women rummaged through these quilts,
talking among themselves as they did so.

"This would be a cutter," one of them mentioned
to the group gathered there.

"Yes, I think so, not much else it would be good
for," another replied.

"Which one?" one woman asked. "I need a cutter
for some patching."

"This fan quilt," the first woman said, "it's in bad
shape from the looks of it."

About that time, someone called out that the
quilts would be sold next. The group of women gathered around, and a few newcomers hurried over as

well, two of them talking quietly to one another. Suddenly, one of them let out a squeal, "Oh, my gosh, Catherine, I can't believe it!"

The other woman exclaimed, "Marcia, did you find it?"

Marcia grabbed hold of a corner of the fan quilt and exclaimed, "Yes, here is my Kiki!"

Seeing the surprised looks on all the other women's faces, Marcia explained who they were.

All the women looked at the newcomers, and one of them said, "If there is something here you wanted, you should have taken it before it was put on the auction block, since these were all of your grandmother's things!"

Marcia replied, "I didn't get into town until today, and I had no idea if the old quilt was even still here! So many of my grandmother's things were stored away. I meant to look for it when I was here for her funeral a few months ago, but there wasn't time. I bought her old trunk just a little bit ago, but the quilt wasn't in it. That is the last place I had seen it when it was still sitting in my grandmother's parlor. The company that handled the auction must have removed it and hung it here with the other quilts from inside the house."

She went on to explain what this quilt meant to her and what her grandmother had done to it on her behalf. She showed them the much used and faded

Kiki block, and explained that that was what she had called her security blanket, because she couldn't say the word "blankie." Kiki had been the word she could pronounce at her young age. At that, the women told her that she'd better be sure to get the quilt, if it meant that much to her. She assured them that it very much did.

"Here comes the auctioneer. He is starting on the quilts now," said Catherine.

When the bidding for the old quilt started, Marcia raised her hand with her bid number held high enough for the auctioneer to see. Moments later, she was hugging the old fan quilt in her arms, having been successful with the opening bid of one dollar.

The quilt was so worn that the auctioneer must have assumed it would not bring a higher price, so he had started the bidding for it at a very low amount. None of the other women who had heard Marcia's story dared bid against her. They all seemed to feel that she was entitled to the long lost memento of her childhood.

As Marcia and Catherine maneuvered through the crowd to put the quilt into the trunk, Marcia said, "Do you know what I am going to do with this old quilt?"

Catherine glanced at her. "What?"

"I am going to cut it up and make Christmas ornaments for all of us—Mom, our brothers, you and me, and maybe even all the rest of our cousins—to have as a keepsake from both our grandmothers."

Catherine agreed, "That would be a wonderful thing to do, since it's beyond repair anyway. Not sure the guys would appreciate it, but their wives will."

Marcia looked it over and said, "Oh, I don't know. I think they might, and I have a feeling that our grandmothers would approve. It sure has seen better days, but I bet if it could talk, it could sure tell some tales. Let's go find Mom and tell her we found it!" She then placed the quilt inside the trunk, closed the lid, and clicked the latch tightly. The two women then retreated through the crowd to find their parents, so they could tell them that what had been lost was now found.

And, so it seems, what goes around, comes around. The old quilt, which had started in bits and pieces, would now be in pieces once again—cut into the shapes of stars and bells, and adorning the Christmas trees of the descendants of Anna and Olinda. These two women, who had made and used the quilt so many years ago, would be remembered each time these ornaments were hung.

Nobody in the family could ever have imagined just how much this quilt had been a part of their family's lives since the day it was created. It had listened to them, watched them grow, and fallen in love with them. It had observed their day-to-day lives, undetected by the human eye, at the hand of something magically unexplained.

As the auction wound down and the crowd had all dispersed, the house sat empty of its contents. A young couple—the mother carrying a tiny baby in a blue blanket as another little boy trailed behind them—was meandering through the yard, talking about what they planned to do with the house now that they had purchased it.

As they walked around, pointing things out to each other, the older child grew restless. He wandered over underneath the old weeping willow tree in the backyard. His father had bought an old coal bucket with a small shovel at the auction, and he asked his parents if he could play with it. They agreed, and soon he was dragging the shovel through a spot of bare dirt under the tree where no grass had grown.

As he dug in the soft earth, a light cool breeze stirred the drooping limbs on the tree, and if you listened closely, you could almost hear the slightest whisper. The little boy looked up, cocking his head as if he had heard something. He saw no one, and went back to his digging.

ACKNOWLEDGMENTS

I am so very grateful to two long-gone family members: my paternal great-grandmother, Anna, and her daughter, Grandma Pearl, who were the inspiration for this book.

I conceived the story not long after I had purchased Great-grandma's trunk at Grandma's auction, with several keepsakes inside. That day, I also acquired a very old quilt, covered with cotton fabric to keep it from falling apart. Removing the fabric revealed the quilt's colorful design. Although it was worn through in places, I made use of the best parts for crafts for my home. As I worked with the pieces, I thought to myself, How old is this quilt? What has it been through in its years of use?

I am sure its original purpose was to cover a bed, but had it also been used to comfort someone when they were sick? Had it been laid on the grass for a picnic, or thrown over an old-fashioned ice cream churn to keep the sun from melting the contents? What would it say if it could tell us of these events?

Much later, over the course of four years, I wrote and rewrote many chapters and added bits of local stories and family legends. It was not my intent to capture my family history, as this story is not specifically about the lives of my ancestors. Still, there are traces of their lives sprinkled throughout the book.

Above all, I thank my husband, Marvin, who put up with my late nights, as I wrote up ideas before they slipped away. Marvin was patient and gracious, and he was my first critic. He knows it has long been my desire to write a book. Whether or not I write another one (I have several ideas), I can cross this off my bucket list of accomplishments.

I am grateful also for the love and support of our children, Matt, Alicia, and Rachel; their spouses, Jen, Tyler, and Mark; and our five grandchildren, Lauren, Emma, Hailey, Abby, Hank, and soon-to-be Baby B. They make my life so much sweeter being their ma-ma.

I appreciate all the input from my mom, Alice, who provided historical insights and proofread the book when I had completed my first draft. She obviously enjoyed it—and had a few laughs over some of the narrative I had incorporated. Yes, our dog really did hide pancakes in my sister's bed! My dad, Jim, who is no longer with us here on earth, would have laughed at that part. I hope you enjoyed it, too.

ABOUT THE AUTHOR

SANDY DUCLOS ECKART has dabbled in writing since she was a teenager and has worked with words for most of her adult life. She has spent 40 years in the health information field, first as a medical records secretary, then as a medical transcriptionist for local and remote hospitals in the United States.

Sandy makes her home in a small southern Illinois community with her husband, Marvin, to whom she has been married for almost four decades. They have three married children and five grandchildren, with another one due in the fall of 2018.

Besides writing, Sandy loves to repurpose rediscovered treasures into home décor, research family genealogy, and read books from several genres.

Grandmother's Fan is Sandy's debut novel.